GOLD WAGON

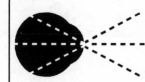

This Large Print Book carries the
Seal of Approval of N.A.V.H.

GOLD WAGON

CHET CUNNINGHAM

WHEELER PUBLISHING
A part of Gale, Cengage Learning

GALE
CENGAGE Learning™

Detroit • New York • San Francisco • New Haven, Conn • Waterville, Maine • London

GALE
CENGAGE Learning

Copyright © 1972 by Chet Cunningham.
Wheeler Publishing, a part of Gale, Cengage Learning.

ALL RIGHTS RESERVED
Wheeler Publishing Large Print Western.
The text of this Large Print edition is unabridged.
Other aspects of the book may vary from the original edition.
Set in 16 pt. Plantin.
Printed on permanent paper.

LIBRARY OF CONGRESS CATALOGING-IN-PUBLICATION DATA

Cunningham, Chet.
   Gold wagon / by Chet Cunningham.
      p. cm.
   ISBN-13: 978-1-59722-741-4 (pbk : alk. paper)
   ISBN-10: 1-59722-741-2 (pbk : alk. paper)
   1. Large type books. I. Title.
PS3553.U468G56 2008
813'.54—dc22   2008003713

Published in 2008 by arrangement with Chet Cunningham.

Printed in the United States of America
1 2 3 4 5 6 7 12 11 10 09 08

GOLD WAGON

CHAPTER ONE

Jim Steel worked the big buckskin up the ravine, letting him pick his way through the clumps of sage and strangled chaparral. He had been climbing toward the ridgeline for nearly two hours, aiming for the Broken Tree Trail into Bisbee.

He had lived in Bisbee for a year once, but now when he thought of the tough little Arizona Territory town, he didn't remember the stifling heat. All he thought about was gold. If his plans went right, that gold would be his. For three months he had been working on this project. Laying the groundwork. Making sure nothing would go wrong.

The fact that Bisbee was still a wild frontier settlement where law and order were near strangers, played a big part in his plans.

Topping the rise, Jim found a smattering of stunted pine and a higher ridge a hundred yards ahead. His eyes automatically scanned the new sweep of ridges and hills to his left and at once he picked up the movement. Half a mile to the east, a lone army scout walked his mount down a ridge. The scout moved deliberately, carefully checking the land on each side of him as he rode; stopping to scan the area ahead.

The buckskin's ears lifted and he snorted as he caught the downwind scent of the other animal. Jim slid down from his horse, running his hand along the animal's snout, catching the nostrils before the buckskin could make another sound.

What was an army scout doing here? Jim checked the lay of the land again, and guessed that the Broken Tree Trail was just over the first rise. Was an army patrol down there? Or could it be an army wagon-train? It was worth a look. Jim tied his neckerchief around the buckskin's jaws and, wrapping the reins over a sage, moved forward as quietly as an Indian.

He was a long rope-throw from the ridge-line when he heard a shot. Automatically he sprawled to the ground, belly down, his six-gun in his hand, his eyes searching. The first shot was followed by a double volley that came from directly in front of him over the ridge.

Jim knew he was shielded from the fire, so

8

he pushed up from the red dust and ran forward, staying low. He was reacting instinctively, from rugged war-time training, and for just a moment it seemed like '63 again. The firing increased now and he heard the scream of a man in pain, and the frightened whinny of a horse. He could hear pistols, the crack of Winchesters and the heavier reports of some Sharps. He skidded to the ground behind a low-growing sage at the crest of the ridge and looked down.

In the arroyo below he saw death and confusion. An army wagon with two teams and a dozen mounted troopers had been ambushed in a gorge a hundred feet wide. Two of the army mounts were down; the escort in near panic.

Two more soldiers fell from their saddles as Jim watched. But where were the ambushers? He studied the far side and spotted them. Four men were dug into the bank, with rock barricades in front of them. He spotted four more positions below him. All eight men were slamming a deadly crossfire into the pony soldiers.

An officer had his saber out and called for his men to dismount to take cover in the rocks, but just as the words left his throat he died in his saddle, his horse galloping away in terror.

The blue coats tumbled off their mounts, crawling for the safety of the boulders. They pulled pistols and fired blindly toward the gully walls, but could see no targets.

A trooper directly below Jim took a bullet in the shoulder as he scampered for the rocks. It tumbled him over but he held onto his pistol. He sat up and holding the gun with both hands fired the rest of his rounds against the bank. Two more rifle slugs jolted into his blue shirt and he screamed, then lay still.

Jim hugged the ground, checking the urge to tear into the fight. But he was older now and smarter. One shot from him and the ambushers would know he was there, and they wouldn't leave a witness to a slaughter like this. He swore to himself, knowing that none of the cavalrymen would survive. It was too neat a trap; the pony soldiers didn't have one chance in hell.

Four of the men scrambled behind boulders. They had protection from one side of the canyon, but didn't seem to realize their backs were exposed from the other side. Quickly they spotted the firing positions on the far bank and began to shoot at them.

Jim bit down hard on the skin of his wrist. He was watching twelve men die and there wasn't a thing he could do to help them! One by one the last of the troopers were picked off.

After the last shot came from the boulders, the attackers remained in their holes. This wasn't a rag-tag outfit, Jim decided, but a closely disciplined group of professionals. The sudden stillness pounded at Jim's ears and his own breathing seemed to boom into the void.

One of the blue shirts in the dirt near the wagon lifted his head and called for help. The only help he received was quick death as two more rifle bullets smashed into his body.

In the long quiet that followed Jim studied the big army wagon. It was a heavy transporter, the kind they used for important shipments from post to post and for gold. The lead team had been shot and were down in the harness, kicking their way toward death. The driver had been hit early, toppling off the seat and falling under the feet of the near team. The two big wagon horses jerked their heads, eyes wild — stamping and skittering as they felt their hooves cutting into the lifeless body of the driver.

Sudden movement to his left caught Jim's attention. A trooper darted from behind a

11

rock, grabbed the saddle horn of an army mount and slapped the horse into action. The gray plunged away, dragging the man. He lifted his feet, dropped them to the ground and swung into the saddle. He was bent low along the horse's neck, but got only twenty yards down the canyon before the bushwhackers found his range. They shot the horse first, killing it before it hit in a dusty roll.

As the dust thinned, Jim saw the soldier crawling toward the dead horse, but he never made it.

Jim concentrated on the hidden riflemen. Some were still half-covered with their ponchos, which in turn had been camouflaged with dirt and rocks. If you didn't know precisely where to look, the ambushers became impossible to locate in the maze of rocks on the steep gully banks.

He understood how the army scout had missed the bushwhackers. They would have heard him coming and vanished under their perfect concealment when he appeared. Jim squinted his eyes against the sun and rubbed the spot on his wrist where he had left tooth marks. Someone had put a lot of planning into this ambush. Who and why?

As he thought about it, he heard a rebel yell across the canyon. Four men on that side and the four on the near slope stood and moved cautiously down the ravine sides. They checked each trooper, making sure every man was dead.

Jim looked back at the wagon. It was the kind he had seen the army use to run gold from the smelters of California to the treasury in Washington. This one was heavily loaded with three-foot sides and canvas tied tightly over the top.

Two of the raiders caught army mounts and spurred away up trail in the direction of the scout. The pony soldier would have heard the firing and be on his way back. He would ride right into the killers and would die too.

The raiders below gathered around the wagon where a big man with a red beard directed them to cut the ropes and pull back the canvas. They began examining each carton, box and sack on board. They ripped open cartons, dumped out the contents, emptied the sacks of flour and grain, scattered boxes of papers and ammunition.

Ten minutes later they had searched every item on the wagon, but had not found what they looked for.

Jim rested his chin on his hand, which lay in the hot dust. So the word was at last out. Somebody else was looking for the ton of gold too. And this bunch didn't mind killing a dozen men to see what was in the wagon.

The men tore at the wagon box, smashing it to pieces with boulders until the sides were demolished and only the bare bed of the rig remained.

On signal the men abandoned the search, stripped guns and valuables from the dead troopers, then caught the army mounts. A rider came in leading seven horses and the killers hit leather. Leading the army nags, they rode off in pairs, each taking a different route away from the massacre. The big red beard was in the last pair to leave. He turned down trail toward Bisbee.

Jim wet his dry lips and stared at the carnage below. There was nothing he could do for the men. The best thing he could do was trail the man with the red whiskers and try to identify him.

Jim let the riders get a quarter of a mile off, then crawled away from the ridgeline toward his horse. A moment later he was astride and riding for Bisbee.

Keeping to the high ground, it was only a few minutes before he spotted the dust of the slow-moving pair of ambushers below him. He cut his speed. It wouldn't be smart to ride down to the trail and overtake them.

But how else could he get close enough to identify them? He thought about it a moment, made his decision, then rode off in the start of a wide arc around the men.

As he rode, Jim pulled the much-folded yellow telegram from his shirt pocket and read it through for the twentieth time.

"Arriving Bisbee 25th with Aunt Abigail. Meet me there." It was signed, "Dan."

When he put it away, Jim's cold blue eyes had more of their normal sparkle. He had been setting up this job for months. "Abigail" was their code word for the army wagon loaded to the axles with gold bars. Now he was sure word had leaked out. But, according to his information, the gold should still be the other side of Bisbee.

He kicked the buckskin into a trot. He continued the wide arc to cut in ahead of the killers. They hadn't seemed in any hurry and with his speed he could get to the big wash just below Bisbee and watch the two men ride past.

He pushed the horse harder now, knowing what he had to do and how to do it. When he hit the opening of the big draw, he pounded hard down the silt-covered floor. Fifty yards from the Bisbee trail, a smattering of brush grew. He eased the horse into the cover and checked the road. He was well hidden, and downtrail he saw a thin line of dust behind two horsemen.

Ten minutes later, Jim watched as the two riders jogged past. One was the large man with the fire-red beard and black hat. The other man was smaller, with a drooping moustache and trail-gray, high-crowned Stetson. Jim memorized the features as they passed.

He let them get half a mile ahead, then rode onto the trail and matched their speed. The two big blacks held a steady pace. Half an hour later he was in Bisbee. It had been two years since he had ridden down this dusty street. There were some new buildings, a gambling hall and a hotel. But it wasn't a homecoming.

The two blacks with sweat streaks stood in front of the Star and Garter, the biggest saloon in town. Jim tied his horse beside them and pushed through the Star's batwing doors. The strong smell of beer, sweat and cigarette smoke in the Star was exactly the same. A dance hall girl at the bar smiled at him. Even Adele was still here. She winked in surprise and started over, but he turned toward the poker tables, not wanting to talk to her yet. She frowned and went back to the bar.

Jim kept his right hand free and low. There

were a dozen men in Bisbee who didn't like him — men from both sides of the law. He had carried a badge here for a year as the town marshal, and that rankled some. He searched the bar and tables. The man with the red beard had discarded his hat, and sat in a poker game with a bottle and glass at his right hand. The big man was completely bald, and hard at work in a hand of five-card stud. His wary eyes were hooded with dark red brows.

For a moment Jim thought he knew the man, but he couldn't be sure. The beard combined with the bald head didn't seem to be the right combination.

The small man stood behind the red beard's chair. He was not over five feet tall, and Jim noticed the way he had his well-worn holster tied low. He would be backing up any play Big Red made. The small man had deep set, dark eyes, and wore a new leather vest — a fancy one — with matching black leather gloves that fit his hands like a second skin.

Jim moved to the bar and edged in beside Adele. She turned toward him slowly.

"Too good for your old friends?" she asked, tilting her head so the long black hair fell loose and inviting around her bared shoulders.

"Never that good, Adele. Any of my other friends still in town?"

"Just the ones you planted in boothill."

"Same old Adele."

"No, smarter, Jim." She lowered her voice. "I want to see you right after closing. About three o'clock at my place, the same one."

Jim ordered a beer, sucked up the foam and a big gulp of the half-cold beer. He hadn't answered her. He shook his head at the beer. "I told Percival if he'd put twice as much straw on those chunks of ice in the ice house he'd keep it half way through summer. He still as pig-headed as ever?"

"Jim, tonight, my place. You be there!" she said.

He turned to look at her, surprised by the emotion in her voice. She was the same: painted lips, rouged cheeks, color under her eyes and a glorious head of black hair. The dress was standard dance-hall modern, tight around the bosom, bare at the shoulders, tight down to the knees where it flared in ruffles and flounces.

"I'll be there, Adele, and I want to know everything that's happened while I've been gone."

He drank the rest of his beer without looking at her. She turned toward the cowboy on the other side.

Jim had just drained his glass, his hand two feet from his gun when he felt the hard muzzle of a six-shooter jammed into his ribs.

"Don't move, kid, and I won't blow a hole through you."

Jim wanted to whirl, to slam down his hand against the gun, but some familiar note in the voice held him. He put his hands down slowly, both on top of the bar, then turned.

"Luke Tabor, you polecat," Jim barked. "You packing the badge here?" Jim shook hands with his old friend and pounded him on the back. "Last time I saw you was in Texas three years ago where you was marshal. They run you out?"

Tabor nodded. "Something like that, Jim. What's your plans?"

"Plans? Just heading through. Going to California. Hear there's a new gold strike out there."

Luke shook his head, his gray eyes steady. "Not you, Jim. I know you better than that. And I keep hearing things from some of our lawman friends. Nobody's got any paper on you yet, understand, but from the talk I hear, you ain't been exactly teaching Sunday School these last three years."

"Always hear talk, Luke."

"Mid-Pacific Railroad, about a year ago.

19

Hear it cost the company fifteen thousand."

Jim grinned. "So I heard. But I don't ride trains much."

"Over in Abilene, that kissing bandit. Took ten thousand and kissed every woman in the bank. He was about your size."

"Sure, about five million other guys are my size too." Jim watched his friend and was surprised how he had aged. Luke was about forty-five, but his short moustache was gray, his sideburns were white and his once-leathery skin was sallow. The gray of his eyes that had been so clear now seemed clouded, and deep lines around his eyes showed too many hard rides.

Jim's voice went lower, concerned.

"They giving you a hard time here, Luke?"

"Things are tough all over."

"Sure. . . ." Jim sensed the tension. "Look, last time we parted we made the promise, remember? If we needed help. . . ."

Luke started to reply, but when he looked past Jim his whole attitude changed, bringing a trace of fear to his eyes.

"Look, I've got to go. Good to see you again, Jim."

He walked quickly toward the front door, leaving without looking at anyone. It was a strange goodbye for men who had sided each other in a dozen shootouts. Jim watched Luke stride past the bat-wings, then searched the room for some unfriendly face. He couldn't say who it was, but Luke had seen someone who turned him into a poor excuse for a man, let alone a sheriff.

Jim scanned the room again, slowly, trying to remember the faces. He saw that the red beard was still at the poker table. But nowhere did he see anything or anyone that could have disturbed the sheriff.

Jim pushed the beer glass away and went outside. Luke had vanished, so Jim took a walk around town. He had just passed the bank and headed for the hotel when a figure came out of the sheriff's office swinging a covered basket and walking toward him. It was full dark now, but the blonde hair spilling from a small hat and the quick, sure stride brought back memories. Was this the little girl he had known before?

Light from the hotel splashed over her as she neared, and he was sure it was Kathy Tabor, Luke's daughter. As she approached, he tipped his hat.

"Miss, I was wondering if you could tell me where there's a hotel in town?"

She paused, cocked her head to one side. She walked a few steps closer to see him better.

"Why yes, the one right behind you is the

best in town," she said. He watched her pretty face frown in confusion. Then her mouth opened in a silent, surprised gasp.

"Oh? Is it really you?"

"Kathy?"

"Yes. Jim?"

"If you're Kathy Tabor, I must be Jim."

"Oh, it's . . . it's so *good* to see you!"

"Just found out you were in town."

"You saw Dad?"

"For a minute, he didn't act like the Luke I used to know."

She stepped closer to him, looking carefully at his face.

"Dad's changed a lot, but so have you. Your face seems stronger now. You look more sure of yourself."

Jim laughed self-consciously. "Well, you're just the same as you were at fifteen, as skinny as a scrub pine post with a hank of yellow hair."

She put her arm through his and handed him the basket.

"I just took Dad his dinner. Can you come to the house with me? I've got a lot to tell you."

"What would the neighbors say?"

She turned, flashing a happy smile at him. "I don't care what those fussy old hens say. Right now I'm so happy I could cry. I didn't think I'd ever see you again."

They walked in silence down the boards, turned left around the bank and on toward the sheriff's house. Jim knew the way, he had lived there for a year himself. As he walked through the door and into the familiar room, he had a warm feeling of belonging.

When Kathy took off the straw hat and shook out her long blonde hair, his breath came with a quick gasp. She was a woman at eighteen — not just grown up — but lovely, beautiful. He wondered why she wasn't married.

She reached out to him and the sense of belonging came over him strongly. It seemed so right. But Jim knew he should leave. He couldn't afford to get involved. If something went wrong with his plans, he and his old friend Luke Tabor could find themselves on opposite sides of the law, with their six-guns roaring.

CHAPTER TWO

"Let me look at you," Jim said, as soon as the lamp had been lighted. She wore a white cotton blouse with ruffles at the high neck and cuffs. A dark green skirt that hadn't come from the bolt-goods of the general store swept almost to the floor from her tiny waist.

"I remember all you did for us, Jim. That time seven years ago when Mother died and you were there. Dad and I just never would have made it. Then three years ago in Lordsville, and . . . and all the other times."

Jim had thought back too. The first time he'd met Luke Tabor had been seven years back, when he had been a marshal in a little backwater called Three Willows. The town fathers found out they couldn't control Luke, couldn't make him forget the law where they were concerned. So they did as they always had — called in two gunfighters.

Jim had ridden in when the two guns braced Luke on Main street. Guns already out, the men told Luke to draw and shoot both ways at once. Jim had left his horse, hit the ground running and called to the gunman at his end. One shot from Jim evened the score, and Luke took care of the other man after taking a slug through the leg. Luke packed up and moved out of town that night before they brought in more guns.

Jim shook his head at the pretty girl. "Kathy, whatever your dad and I did for each other has balanced out."

"No, Jim. That isn't true. We're in your debt much more. And now we need help again. I guess the Tabors need lots of help."

"Kathy, what's wrong?"

"The man who killed Mama. He's here in town, Jim. He keeps laughing at Papa, making fun of him. He teases Papa to draw. This afternoon he gave Papa a week to get out of town. You know what that's doing to Luke Tabor."

Jim scowled at the fireplace as he lit the fire that had been laid there. He had to think. He didn't come to town to hold the hand of some sheriff who was over the hill. He now understood the look in Luke Tabor's eyes. He was scared, bone-weary from too many nights on the ground; tired out from too many long rides after outlaws who could ride longer and faster; sick at heart at man's inhumanity to man. He should not be a sheriff any longer, or somebody would gun him down.

Ten years ago, or even five years ago, if some man told Luke Tabor to get out of town Luke would have gunned him on the spot or broken him up with his two bare hands.

Jim came back and sat down at the dining room table across from Kathy. Her eyes were brim full of tears.

"Who is the man? You say the one who killed your mother, but I thought. . . ."

"So did Papa until four months ago. Then Red Paulson stormed into town and began taking over. He calls Bisbee his town, and it just about is. He never pays for anything, has a room at the hotel and never pays them a cent. And he has plenty of money."

She touched her handkerchief to her eyes.

"You wouldn't know Red now. He lost almost all of his hair when he got sick, he says, so he shaved the rest off and grew a long red beard. . . ."

Jim stood up quickly. "And does he ride with a short man with a fast gun, kind of slick and snake-looking?"

"You've seen them. They hang out at the

Star and Garter most of the time, drinking and gambling."

Jim grabbed his hat and checked his .44. It had five rounds in the cylinder with the hammer setting on the empty.

"Kathy, I might have something that will help your father. It's something I should have told him before. I'm not promising anything."

At the door he tipped his hat, but Kathy reached out a slender hand and took his.

"Jim, don't just ride away from me again, promise?" She blushed as she thought what she had said. Her smile was a little crooked now. "I've never been good at lying, or covering up my feelings. So please be careful, and please stop by and see me."

When the soft white hand touched his rope-roughened one, he felt a strange lift. No woman's touch had ever done that to him before. Just so it didn't get in the way of his date with Abigail. And helping Luke might be a step to helping himself. Quickly he touched his hat and closed the door. He almost ran to the street, then held himself down to a steady walk toward the sheriff's office.

Luke wouldn't be in the office this time of night. He'd be out checking on the gaming houses and the fancy-women hotels on

27

Front Street. But when Jim grabbed the handle of the sheriff's door, it was unlocked, and he pushed in easily.

"Yeah?"

Jim saw no one in the office. He found the voice coming from a man in the first cell.

"Sheriff in?"

"Nope, and that's a fact."

Jim saw the man push up on one elbow on the bunk. The cell door wasn't locked.

"Know where he is?"

"Nope and that's a fact."

"Thanks for your help," Jim said and left. He tried four saloons, but didn't find Luke. He saved the Star and Garter till last, but Luke wasn't there either. The idea of a good supper crossed Jim's mind, but he decided to settle for a beer instead, then find the sheriff.

Jim had downed half the mug of lukewarm beer when he remembered the telegram. He pulled it out, read it again and pushed it back into his pocket before asking the bartender the date.

"Us that can read, cowboy, know it's June 25, 1866. That's a Tuesday."

Jim reached for his drink, and as he did two men moved quickly beside him, pinning his arms on the high bar — a gun muzzle jammed into his ribs for the second time that night.

"Don't even wiggle, Kid. Harry's trigger finger's been a mite fast lately."

Jim looked up at the mirror backing the bar and saw the red beard first, then the glistening pate of Red Paulson. The man with the gun must be Harry. Slowly, Jim reached for his glass of beer and lifted it to his mouth.

"What's with you and the sheriff, Kid? Harry says you and him looked like long-lost cellmates."

Jim set down the glass and wiped the foam off his lips. He ignored the gun, and Paulson.

"Hey, don't I know you from somewhere?" Red went on. "Kansas maybe, five, six years back? You was younger then, a real kid." Red looked at Jim again, then shrugged. "Damned if I know, Kid. Least you wasn't one I beat the draw on." He laughed with a high cackle. "Little joke there, Boy." His voice changed.

"Now, look, Kid. I don't like our sheriff, see. This is my town and I run it like I want. Anybody who backs Luke Tabor, goes up against me first. Savvy?"

For the first time Jim turned toward the larger man, his blue eyes slashing at the red

29

beard. "I'd like that, like to go up against just you in an honest showdown. With Harry sitting on his hands."

Red bristled. "You in a rush to die, Kid. You leave that Tabor alone and grow old."

Jim had been burning inside during the talk. At last he couldn't take it any more. His elbows lashed out to each side, blasting into Red Paulson's chest and grazing Harry's shoulder. Jim followed with a roundhouse right that caught Paulson behind the ear and dropped him to his knees. Jim whirled to find Harry, when the gun butt slammed down hard on his skull and he remembered nothing more.

When Jim came to, it was slowly, like he was wading through a deep fog, or trying to fight his way up through a mile of foam to the top of the water so he could get a deep breath. His lungs felt like they were burning. He groaned and tried to roll over, but strong hands held him.

One eye came open, blinked at the raw light of the kerosene lamp and closed again. He forced it open and made out the wallpaper on the ceiling, an odd pattern of birch trees and riders going over low fences. Crazy.

"Jim, wake up. You've slept long enough

on this drunk. Now come on, Jim, sober up." The voice had a ring of command, and he tried to get his other eye open. He should know the voice. He realized he was on a bed, not in the dirt of some alley.

He sniffed and the faint odor of lavender came through. That was when Jim knew where he was. Adele. He blinked open both eyes and stared at the black-headed girl.

"No, how in the. . . ."

"Quiet!" Adele said. She had wrapped white bandages around his chest and every time he breathed, it hurt. His head pounded like a freight train was roaring through it.

"Just relax, you're safe for a while. When you tore into Red and Harry, I got the word, and did a little stomping of my own with a Greener shotgun to back up my play. Now listen careful to what I say. Luke Tabor helped me get you over here, no, this ain't my place, just the same kind of wallpaper. Nobody'll bother you here till morning. By then you got to be well enough to decide how far you're going to ride and how fast. Red don't take to cowboys knocking him down, not unless he can even things up with a wooden marker on boothill."

"Adele, I'm not dead. What'd he do, stomp me?"

"Some. Now listen. I know you're in town

for that wagon supposed to be coming through. You and half a dozen other outfits planning on taking it between here and the rail-head. Me included. Now I've got a plan, and six men, but if we could weed out some of the competition it would help."

"What wagon?"

"You know damn well what wagon. The wagon coming from California with the ton of gold. Don't play games with me, Jim. I been hoping you'd show up to lead my hand."

"Crazy, government sends all the gold north of here. Why bring it way down here? And I don't know what you mean by a gold wagon. I heard Luke Tabor needed help, so I come in. Where am I, anyway?"

"Lucy's Hotel, you know the spot."

He knew it, the fanciest, highest-priced bordello in town, with confidential entrances to half the rooms.

"Damn, been a long time since I been here."

"Well, I couldn't take you to my place, that's the first spot Red will look."

"And then Luke's place."

"Yes, but you're not going anywhere. Way I figure it, your helping out Luke will have to wait. I saved that no good hide of yours tonight. Red wouldn't have stopped Harry

Zedicher from kicking your head in."

"Harry *Zedicher?*"

"Yeah, you heard of him?"

"Once or twice." He tried to sit up, but the pounding took over in his head again. He settled for pushing in on his ribs and decided none of them were broken. He'd show bruises for a few weeks. So, nothing broken. He looked at the dresser and saw his gun belt with the Colt still in place.

"Adele, I should kiss you."

"Go ahead, it wouldn't be the first time."

He leaned up and kissed her red lips, then settled back with a groan.

"Was that me, cowboy, or the paste on the head you got?"

When his head stopped spinning he just grinned.

She stood up. "Remember, I get first call on that gun of yours. As near as I can tell the wagon was delayed three days getting out of California. They sent out four dummy wagons, and claim jumpers wiped out two of them, I heard, with nothing for their trouble but some army horses and shooting irons. The target date for Bisbee was today, the 25th, right? but it didn't come, so we get ready for three days from now."

He nodded.

"Now don't go away. Meet you at Ma

Parson's cafe first thing in the morning, about eight."

Jim nodded once more and closed his eyes. He heard her start to say something, then listened to her steps as she went out of the room quietly.

Jim sat up slowly, beating down the pounding. He felt the back of his head and found the square patch someone had taped to his scalp. It took a tremendous effort to get his feet worked around so he could put them on the floor. Once he almost passed out, but he held his head low until it cleared.

It took him ten minutes to get to the window. He was on the first floor back. Many a good man had vaulted out that window in the dead of night. He'd be doing good if he could fall out of it. He walked shakily back to the dresser and put on his gunbelt. Never before had he felt the weight of the Colt and the line of ammunition. Tonight it felt like a ton of lead dragging him to his knees.

The window opened easily, but the effort made his chest heave and the injured ribs yowled in pain, pulling a groan from him. He put his right foot over the sill, then lifted up his left as he hugged the open window. He would ordinarily have rolled over on his stomach, pushed away and dropped to the ground, but he knew if he rested his weight on his chest he'd pass out.

Cautiously he ducked under the window with his head and shoulders, and pushed away. He couldn't see the ground. It rushed up at him like a runaway bronc and when he hit, he tumbled forward on his hands and knees. The shock of the sudden stop drove his head to a frenzy and almost made him faint again, but he fought back, shaking his head gently, lowering it to pull more blood into it, and at last he weathered the fight.

He sat down, resting, and five minutes later struggled to his feet and walked slowly down the alley to the dusty street beyond. He didn't know where he was going, but it was away from the whorehouse. Adele said there were half a dozen bands after the wagon. He wondered if they all knew as much about it as he did, he doubted it. He had a man who was either with the wagon or one of the last enlisted men to see the gold before it was moving over the trails. The code name of Abigail was his clue, his lead, and so far it had led him straight down the line toward a ton of gold. A ton of gold, worth more than a half a million dollars! It was more money than he possibly could imagine. His room would cost him a dollar for the night. He could get a good meal for fifty cents, and a fine hand-gun for twenty dollars. A half a million was unthinkable.

He paused at the street and glanced both ways. He had to see the sheriff. Had to tell him about the slaughter of the army unit and who had done it. If he could get Red Paulson and his army out of the way, it would simplify matters.

He made two detours, used another alley and came up behind the county jail. It was a solidly built building next to the courthouse, and he knew where the key used to be kept. The door led only into a storage room and from there to a locked door that went into the aisle between the six cells.

He found the key, twisted it in the lock and slid inside. It was dark inside, no one saw him. A moment later he was pounding on the door that led into the jail.

For a moment he thought all the struggle had been in vain. He heard the low laugh of Red Paulson just behind him and felt two strong hands band around his throat. For the second time in hours Jim felt the blackness of unconsciousness sweeping over him. Furiously he pulled at his Colt and fired directly in front of him. He heard a gasp of pain, then a scream ending in a soft bubbling sound, as the hands around Jim's throat loosened and fell away. Jim staggered to one side and leaned quickly against the wall. He heard footsteps moving toward the back of the room. A shaft of moonlight cut into the blackness of the storage area as the back door was jerked open. It was too dark to be certain, but Jim was sure he saw the moonlight gleaming off the bald dome of Red Paulson as he ran into the alley.

CHAPTER THREE

Jim heard the shouts from the jail, then as the key scraped in the big lock, he tried to move away from the door he knew would be swung open hard. He almost made it by crawling. The door caught only his right foot as it blasted open. Someone held a lamp high in one hand, and a six gun low in the other.

"What in hell?" Luke Tabor growled as he saw Jim on the floor.

The light bounced off a fancy leather vest and as Jim turned he saw what he had crawled over — Harry Zedicher. Jim had seen enough dead men to know Harry would never draw again. Luke took one look at the gunman and turned to Jim.

"You all right, Boy?"

"I'll live." He glanced at the dead man, then at his own gun still smoking. "How did Zedicher get in here?"

Luke took a jail blanket and spread over

the body, then checked Jim's battered face.

"He came in same way you did. No secret where the key is. I'd say he was waiting for you. I just don't understand how you shot him first."

Jim stood up painfully. "You heard he stomped me. Harry and Red knew Adele took me out, maybe they figured I'd come back here to talk to you. They figured right. Harry was trying to choke me. My guess is Harry didn't figure I could put up much of a fight and wanted to finish me quietly."

"What now?"

"You want Red Paulson behind bars waiting for army justice?"

Luke laughed bitterly. "I'd give my right arm for that."

"Then take a posse and head out Broken Tree Trail. I know it isn't used much, but I came over it yesterday. I saw Red Paulson and seven men ambush an army convoy and wipe it out. Ten mounted men and two on the wagon. I saw the whole thing and I'll testify in court. Now I hope you've got a spare cell where I can get some sleep."

They put the only mattress in the cell over the rough boards of the bunk and found blankets. Then Luke caught at Jim's sleeve.

"It's true, what you said about Red?"

"It's true."

"You know who he is?"

"Yes, Wilsonville, seven years ago. I talked to Kathy."

"She, ah, she say anything about me?"

"Little bit."

"I'm not as fast as I used to be, Jim. Sure would like to have you as my deputy for the next couple of weeks."

"I'm through playing lawman, Luke. Last town I worked they indicted me for murder. I beat the charge, and then I swore I'd never be a lawman again. It's a thankless job, and a dangerous one. You should know that."

"Right, Jim, right. But this time, we've got a chance to nail that damned Red! You got to help me! You remember how he charged into the house that night, shooting with both hands. You know he could have stopped when he was sure I wasn't there but he went right ahead and 'accidentally' killed my Martha. I'd been looking for him, Jim. Then my joints started to go sour. Can't hardly hold a gun no more. Watch."

He pulled his gun from the holster, almost dropped it, then got his trigger finger into the housing. Jim looked in surprise at the twisted fingers. One stuck straight out and wouldn't bend.

"Some fancy sawbones said it was arthritis, or something like that. Nothing he could do, he said."

Jim stared at the crooked hand again, but the only thing he could see was Red Paulson calling out Luke some night when he was through playing cat and mouse. Luke would die. Too proud not to go out, too scared and too hurt to get his gun from the holster. Then the town would really belong to Paulson. Even a wild, wide-open town like Bisbee deserved better than a Red Paulson at the throttle.

"Lock both doors and get some sleep," Jim told Luke. "I won't take a badge, but I'll hang around for a week or so and help you with Paulson. First thing it gets daylight have three more men ready and we'll ride out to that ambush site."

Red Paulson staggered against the back of the hotel and leaned there, panting for breath. He hadn't run that far in two years. He gulped in lungsful of air, puffing hard like a steam engine. Damn, where did Jim get that gun? He should have played it smart and let Zedicher kill Steel outside. Why did he try to play it so cute?

Red had learned who Jim was a half hour after Adele had hoisted the Greener and backed everybody off. He might have been able to beat Adele, but shooting a woman, even one holding a shotgun on you, just wasn't the thing to do. He'd be run out of town so fast he wouldn't have time to stop for his extra cartridges.

But just knowing that Jim Steel was the same one who sided Luke Tabor up in Kansas was enough to get him and Harry moving again. Red hadn't even bothered to look at Harry. He heard that .44 roar and an instant later that last long breath gush out of the little gunnie and he knew it was all over for him. He hated to lose a good man — Harry was one of the best.

Now he had to wring out of Adele why she sprang Steel from the trap Harry had him in. There was a nagging hunch in the back of his mind the girl may have wanted Jim to use on her own. Could she know about the gold wagon coming through? He put the idea aside as he walked on to the back door of the Star and pushed inside. Adele was supposed to be working. If she wasn't, he'd find her. He would have trouble enough with the army guard around that gold wagon, he didn't want one or even two other gun outfits to fight too.

Adele wasn't in the Star and Garter. She wasn't upstairs with a man. Lenny, the barkeep, said she went home sick about an hour ago. She'd really be sick when he found her, Red thought. She was the one gal in the Star he hadn't been able to touch. If he found her tonight he'd touch her plenty.

Five minutes later he was outside the door of the small house built toward the middle of the block and behind another house. It had been built years ago for a maiden sister. Now Adele owned it and the house in front which she rented. Some of these whores had more money than anyone suspected, Red thought, as he eased up and looked in the lighted window.

Adele sat in a rocking chair, a tabby cat on her lap and a six-gun in her hand. She was sound asleep.

Red grinned as he tested the window. It was not locked, now if it would open without a sound he would be in luck. The sound the wood scraping on wood made was slight as he pushed the window up. He went through it quickly and closed it, pulling the blind all the way down. Two soft steps later, he eased the heavy Colt from Adele's fingers. He watched her a moment, then smoothed the cat's fur. His other hand reached up and stroked the dress where it covered her full breasts.

Adele awoke with a small cry strangled in her throat. He had jumped back and held the Colt loosely.

"Well, Adele. Thought it was about time you and I had a good, long talk. Now don't scream, we wouldn't want your tenants to get excited, would we?"

"Get out!"

"I only just got here, so that wouldn't be neighborly of me, now would it? Besides, I've never seen you naked. I bet you've got a good body underneath all those ruffles and frills."

"You'll never know."

"Strip, Adele, take them all off."

"No, not in a million years."

"Don't think Jim is coming to rescue you. Harry just killed him in the jail storeroom where he was hiding. So come on, take them off."

"I don't believe you."

Red took out a knife and opened it, snapping the blade in place. He touched the finely honed blade, then tested it by shaving off some hair on his arm. It was sharp as a razor.

"Saw a little gal in St. Louis once. She was in a two-bit flop house with no takers. Poor thing was skin and bones but the interesting part was her face. Had a man's initials carved in her cheeks. A big 'B' on one cheek and a big 'C' on the other.

44

Somehow they never healed good, red welts stood out like a new moon on a clear night." He walked toward her, the knife ready.

"Now we wouldn't want anything like that to happen to Adele, would we?" The knife moved down and sliced through the strap holding up the dance-hall dress. Adele gasped. The thin blade pressed flatly against her cheek.

"We wouldn't want anything to happen to those soft, pretty cheeks, would we?"

Adele shivered, looked toward the hand that held the blade and sighed. "What do you want, Red?"

"You know."

"What else?"

"We'll get to that." He pushed the other shoulder strap off and started to pull down the top of her dress.

"I'll do it," she said.

Red Paulson grinned and watched the dress come off.

"You're damn right you will," he said.

The five horsemen rode easily in the quietness of dawn. Behind them came a flat-bed wagon pulled by a sturdy team. The trail they were on led to the northwest, curling around ravines and rocks, becoming smaller and less defined as they continued. It was a rugged wagon track over the low hills and not much used now. Jim wondered why the wagon had come in this direction. The army was trying a wild set of decoys for the real gold wagon.

The army would be notified as soon as the sheriff confirmed the deaths. But the men would have to be buried on the spot, with crude wooden markers for the army board of inquiry to look at when it got there. Jim hated this kind of work. He always had as a lawman, now with so many bodies to bury it would be rugged, hot work before the graves were finished. He decided he would let Luke collect any identification left on the men.

They rode for two hours with little talk. The sun brimmed the hills and bore down on them, hot, surly, as if it were trying to slow them down.

They saw the birds circling high while the posse was still a mile away. The big birds made their tight circles, then came down, down, until they were lost from sight over the ridge.

The trail was little used. Jim remembered it was the old trail before the new wagon road had been put through. Now it carried a few horsemen. That was probably why no one had stumbled on the bodies.

As they topped the last rise the sheriff called a halt so they could look down at the scene. Jim noticed Luke had taken out a folded piece of paper and a stub pencil and was drawing a rough sketch of the area, showing the hills, the wagon, the position of the dead men and horses. When he finished they moved down to the slaughter. Luke worked methodically, taking identification from any men who had it, noting their approximate age and rank. When he finished, the other men dug graves and laid the soldiers in them. By noon they were done, the graves marked only with mounds of stone so the coyotes wouldn't dig up the bodies.

Luke sat on a stone, making the last notes on his folded sheet of paper.

"Not much left of the wagon," Jim said, leaning on a shovel.

Luke stood and together they walked to the battered remains. They had stripped the harness from the dead animals and put it on the town wagon. Only the tongue and the bed remained over the wheels.

"Sombody was looking for something," Luke said.

"Payroll?"

"Gold," Luke said softly, not looking up. "And it's crossed my mind, Jim, that you probably know more about the shipment than I do."

"How would I know anything about gold?"

"Ways, Jim. We've had men drifting into town for a week. First thing they do is look up a calendar and find out what the date is. Now wouldn't you say that was a little out of the ordinary for a cowpoke or even a saddle bum?"

Jim nodded.

"Gold, Jim. That's what draws them. This must have been a decoy."

They walked back toward their horses.

"Now, Jim, show me where you were when you saw them, and let's take a look at the way the bushwhackers were dug in."

An hour later they pushed out behind the wagon. They had pulled the big heavy wheels off the hulk of an army wagon and loaded them aboard the town rig. Now the two horses earned their oats as they dragged the rig behind them.

"Jim, I don't know why you come to town, but that girl of mine was singing when I got home last night. She looked as bright and happy as a just-nursed calf." He looked up, and reset his hat on his gray head, squinting his eyes against the glare of the uncompromising sun. "Now, I don't really care why you came to town, but I'm at a point where I need some help."

He turned and there was a pleading in his eyes that Jim had never seen in a man before. It was a soul-ripping, gut-simple scream for aid. The window to the very soul of Luke Tabor closed and a thin veneer of toughness covered it.

"What I need is a deputy, somebody I can count on who Red Paulson won't scare off the first day. I need your gun behind me."

Jim scratched his dark hair under his hat and adjusted it before answering. "Luke, I never had much luck wearing a badge."

"Jim, how can I bring in Red Paulson and his whole gang? Eight of them you said. My gun can't even equal Red's, let alone six more now that Shorty Zedicher is gone."

"I really don't see how I can help you, Luke. I've got some business of my own that just can't wait."

When Jim looked ahead, a chill shot through his spine. The old trail cut through a gully, with forty-foot banks on each side. It reminded him too much of the place they had just left. He asked Luke to hold up the procession.

"How many men did you talk to last night before you got the posse?"

"Oh, about ten or twelve. Most of them

wanted nothing to do with the idea."

"That's what I was afraid of," Jim said scowling. "Hold everyone here until I show up at the other end of that wash."

Luke looked at the sides of the arroyo and nodded.

Jim had ridden a hundred yards at right angles to the trail, then cut down-trail again and spurred his mount up the side of the razorback the runoff water had cut through. He saw the first man lying on the ground looking into the ravine. A rifle lay at his side.

But it was too late to rein up or to go back. The man turned and snapped a shot at Jim with his six-gun. Jim had the big Sharps out of the scabbard, levered a round into the chamber and sighted down on the bushwhacker. The heavy report of the rifle boomed through the desert silence. Jim saw the man jolt as the slug ripped into him, then lay still.

Jim had no time to think about it. Two more men ran over the low rise, rifles ready. He could only kick away from the horse as he jumped for the ground, the Sharps gripped tightly to his chest. He hit hard, rolled once and zig-zagged toward a handful of boulders twenty feet away, as his buckskin clattered away downhill.

He lay behind the rocks, safe for the moment, knowing he was shielded from the ambushers. He wondered if Luke had heard the shots. He had a moment to think about the guns in front of him. The odds could be six to one, half of that if Red had positioned men on both sides of the gully. And it had to be Red and his bloody crew. Who else would bushwhack a posse?

The first slug slapped against the rock in front of him and whined off into the bright blue sky. Jim felt better then, like when the first shot of a battle came and it had begun. He settled down to watch around the boulder and wait for his first move. It was a deadly game of cat and mouse he knew very well, probably as well as any man alive.

CHAPTER FOUR

Jim checked the surrounding area, automatically finding the next cover and a route to get to it in case he had to leave the rocks. It came from rugged training and two years of fighting to stay alive as General Sherman swept his way to the sea. In those days you learned what to do fast or died trying.

Jim watched a clump of bush near the top of the razorback. His Sharps came up and he sighted in carefully. The same brush moved again and he fired. The man who had been crouched there pitched forward, a surprised expression on his face as his hands tried to stop the torrent of red that gushed from his chest. Jim moved to the other side of the clump of big rocks and surveyed the hill above. He saw no movement. Two shots blasted into the air from beyond the crest of the hill. Pistol shots, he guessed. Was it a signal?

He eased back to the center of the twin

rocks and peered through the slot where they met. The top of the hill and both his flanks were quiet. A moment later he knew why. Four riders suddenly galloped full bore over the hill and directly at him. It took him a few precious seconds to get the Sharps up. The first blast brought down the lead horse. By the time he had reloaded, the riders were coming past the rocks. He caught the first one in the shoulder with the Sharps smashing him off the horse.

Something burned his right arm and he spun around, falling against the rock and rolling. His six-gun came into his hand — he fired twice at the rider taking aim at him from the right. Both shots missed. But the rider suddenly folded in half and slid off his mount. The man dropped almost at Jim's feet.

Four! Four! The word burned in his brain as he leaped toward the dead man's horse. The mount had been well gun-trained, and when the reins went slack, he stopped. Jim leaped on board the black, grabbed the reins and spurred down the hill. He was just in time to see the fourth horseman making a wide arc away from him and being chased by Luke Tabor.

Jim read the story in an instant. Luke's horse had four hours of riding already, the outlaw horse was fresh. Luke would never catch the quarry, but might ride into a trap.

Jim raised his six gun and shot three times quickly, and Luke looked back, caught Jim's arm wave and broke off the chase.

When the five men gathered at the body of the last victim Jim held out his hand to Luke.

"Thanks, Luke, he had me cold."

Luke snorted. "He shoulda had you the first time. Know him?"

They turned the man over and stared at his face. No one knew him. The other three dead men were also strangers, and Jim was sorry none of them sprouted a red beard.

"Got to be some of Red's men," Luke said when the bodies had been tied down to the flat-bed wagon. They found three horses and tied them to the wagon. If nobody claimed them within a month they would be sold and the money put in the city treasury.

"That leaves Red with three gun-hands," Luke said as they rode a quarter of mile ahead of the wagon, carefully checking any new ambush spot.

"Maybe. But if he could hire eights guns, he can hire five more to replace what he lost. Where does he get his money?"

Luke shook his head. "Beats me. I tried to

54

figure it out once a month ago, but I got box canyons every time."

"Somebody in town? Does he seem to be an enforcer for some ranch outfit, or some saloon? How about the Star and Garter? Could he be working for Percival?"

"That's an idea I didn't chew over before."

Luke kept quiet until they were almost to town. Then he looked up with one last appeal.

"I still need that deputy, Jim. Throw in with me for a week. That's enough time to take care of Red and his bunch." Luke's gray eyes were insistent, pleading. "For old time's sakes, Jim. You still owe me for Lordsburg, and this morning too. It coulda been your carcass stretched out on that wagon."

Jim was surprised that Luke would go so far. There must not be a man in town who would back him with a gun. Jim thought of the telegram. With Red and his bunch out of the way it would be much simpler.

At last he nodded at Luke. "I'll back you, Luke, but not as a deputy. I back you when I can, and when it's time to move — out I go, no questions asked."

Luke nodded and blinked quickly to keep an old man's tears out of his eyes. "Thanks, Jim. I'm beholden to you."

■ ■ ■ ■

When they rode into Bisbee a trail of people followed them. Four bodies on a wagon loaded down with army wagon wheels and a pair of harnesses made an odd load. They stopped in front of the preacher's house. He also served as the town's undertaker. Luke lined the bodies up on the boardwalk.

"Now take a look at these four. Any of you know any of them, let me know. These men tried to bushwhack our posse and I want to know why."

He stood back and two dozen men passed in front of the men, talking about the bodies but not about their names. It seemed no one knew any of the dead, would-be killers.

After half an hour Luke signaled the undertaker who had the bodies moved into the back of his shop. The next day they would be buried on the far side of the city cemetary, the free side. Sale of the horses would just about pay for the burying charges.

After Luke and Jim had walked through town to the sheriff's office, Jim had a question.

"You going to bring in Red Paulson to-day?"

"Not sure. It's his word against yours that he was at that massacre, and the judge might let him off."

"But that attack today, that had to be Red."

"Sure, Jim, sure it was, but prove it? We can't. All we can do is guess — no judge is going to hold still for that kind of evidence."

Jim swore softly. Luke was right, there was no doubt about that. They needed solid evidence.

"Let me go bring him in anyway," Jim said smiling at Luke. "You know he won't come, and we can save the county the cost of a trial."

Luke shook his head. "Then I'd have to lock you up for a trial, Jim. Now, if you'd take a badge, it'd be a different color of scalp-lock."

Jim shook his head and poured a cup of coffee from the pot on the small wood-burning stove.

"Notified the army about their lost men?"

"On the morning stage. It's two days to the fort from here."

"So we've got no help from them for at least four days. Maybe a week," Jim said.

Jim was ready to leave when the door

opened, and a long gingham skirt rustled into the office as Kathy Tabor came in, the same basket on her arm he had seen the night before.

"Hi Dad, hello, Jim."

She turned toward him and he wanted to catch his breath, she was so beautiful. She was smiling that special way she used to, when she was fifteen and told him someday she would marry him.

"Fried chicken, Jim? I brought plenty for two. Saw you come into town, and I hoped you'd still be here." She began to spread a cloth on her father's desk and put out the chicken.

"We've got some muffins and currant jelly, and some cherry pie if you're hungry for it," she said stepping back.

Jim touched her shoulder, a smile blooming on his face he couldn't control. "You remembered about the chicken! Remember how we used to catch those white leghorns and wring their necks and get them ready to fry?"

Luke had watched the exchange with a cautious eye. He seemed to relax a little and turn sassy. "You two remember all you want, just don't hog all the chicken!"

"Are you going to be Daddy's deputy?"

"Kathy, now I don't think. . . ."

"Dad, I want to know, so I'll ask. If you two are not up to counting up the favors, I certainly am."

Jim put down the piece of chicken he had stripped half the meat from and chewed it. Suddenly he wasn't hungry any more. He stood up and grabbed his hat.

"If you want to count it up and run a sum, Kathy, you better add one more on your dad's side. Luke saved my life not two hours ago." Jim turned sharply and went out the door, not seeing the look of surprise, shame and confusion that flooded across the pretty girl's face.

Jim felt the powder-flash of his anger cooling almost before he had closed the door, but he wasn't going back in there and apologize. Come to think of it she always had had a quick temper. Many times they had ended a meeting by shouting at each other.

He marched across the street toward the one-story court house and found the county clerk's office on the back row of offices. After getting permission of the clerk on duty, he began looking at maps of the county, then of the Territory of Arizona. At last he checked a map of the whole country, from California to the Atlantic ocean.

He was checking alternate routes the

wagon might have taken since leaving California. It certainly was a long way out of a direct line toward the railroad head. He guessed there would be about three wagons, maybe four, but with only a small escort of not over a dozen blue-coats. The pony soldiers probably wouldn't know what was in their wagons.

As he put the maps up the clerk came back.

"Sure is a big country, isn't it?"

Jim nodded.

"Seems more folks been looking at them roll-down maps lately. Why just this morning Mr. Paulson was in and looked at that Arizona map for nigh onto an hour."

Jim turned, frowning. "He here all morning?"

"Oh, no, he left about nine, and rode out northwest. I wondered about it at the time, cause the only thing up that way is the schoolhouse and the Broken Tree trail."

"And you're sure it was before nine this morning?"

The little man looked up, grinned and nodded. "That it was. I always time myself on everything." He pulled out a pocket watch attached to his vest by a silver chain. "Yes, sir, it was exactly 8:55, because I was getting ready to go through the morning

60

correspondence."

"And your name, sir?"

"Randolph J. Jones. I was working here when you were our sheriff back three years. That's why I let you look at the maps. You going to be working with the new sheriff?"

Jim hardly heard the question. He shook his head and walked out of the office, trying to pin down a fleeting idea that had come to him suddenly, brushed past his mind and flown off. At least he had a witness who could swear Red went up the Broken Tree trail this morning before the ambush.

He shook his head as he stood on the board walk, watching the mid-day traffic. Twice as many teams and wagons and horses in town as there were three years ago. He didn't see why. This was a town born of want and living in poverty. It had no reason for its existence at all.

He looked across the street and through the clutter of stores and offices. On the next block he could see a paintless house with a weathervane on the roof — a large sheet-metal rooster turning with the changeable wind. That was the house owned by Adele, who must have the distinction of being the oldest dance-hall girl in the Star and Garter. When he was in town before, he'd heard she'd been there ten years.

How did Adele learn about the gold wagon? And just how much did she know? It was time he paid her an unofficial call. He grinned. An unprofessional call.

When he knocked on Adele's door, he heard only a groan and a shout to go away. He knocked louder, then tried the door. It was locked. He pounded harder.

At last the door opened three inches, held in place by a bolt and chain.

"Yeah?"

"Adele, Jim. I want to talk to you."

"Jim Steel!" she said before the door swung open. "Come in, I want to talk to you!"

Adele was a mess. Her hair fell in strings over her shoulders, her face was a chalky white and her eyes still smudged from last night's paint.

"I'm not keeping you from your sleep?"

"Hell no. I sleep too much, I get fat, and you know what they say about fat girls?"

He laughed and she waved it aside. "Where in hell were you all night, and then this morning? We had a date in the cafe, remember? I busted a lacing to get up to that greasy spoon and you weren't there."

He told her what he had been doing about that time and she looked like she was going to be sick.

"So the army sent out another dummy? That's three that's come through here. Now what wiped them out?"

"Yes."

"So tell me."

"No. I worry about the competition. Now how do you know about the gold?"

Adele laughed. She was wearing a long robe which she evidently had thrown on over a long ruffled night-gown. She flipped aside the robe top until it exposed the curve of her breast.

"Oh, a girl has ways."

"I know about the ways, remember? What I want to know is who you were sleeping with when you found out."

She didn't blush or cringe and pretend to be shocked.

"We're laying our cards on the table?"

"Right out in sight."

She dropped the robe and kicked it toward the wall.

"Ed Percival. He's not cut out for this kind of work. He runs a good gambling hall and saloon, but the heavy stuff is too much for him. The dummy talked in his sleep!"

"And you listened."

"No, Jim, I didn't just listen, I asked him

questions and he answered me. The next night I found out some more and some more until I had all the pieces."

"And now you're out for the gold."

"Why not? I could open my own place, run my own saloon and gambling hall."

"You're going to look funny going up against thirty army rifles trying to get that yellow."

"There aren't thirty, there are only. . . ." she stopped and laughed. "Nothing is free around here, cowboy. Do you want to sign on my crew or not?"

"I'd have to know a lot more about your crew. Who are they? What have they done before? And will they shoot us both in the back and take off with the gold?"

"First we get it, then we worry about each other. I've got six men I'm paying a dollar a day to sit and wait for that wagon of gold. If you'll ramrod my boys, I'll pay you two dollars a day, and twenty percent of everything we get."

"How many outfits in town waiting for that wagon?"

"Only you, and one other I know of."

"Besides Percival. Red Paulson and his boys working for Percival?"

"Not that I know of. I don't know where he will get his guns from when the time is right." As he watched, Adele untied the ribbon holding the top of her nightgown together.

"Well, Jim, it's time to decide. Are you with me or against me?" She pulled the loose nightgown off her shoulders letting it drop to her waist. "Jim, darling, don't be so stuffy, I can offer you lots of things. Why not sign on with me?"

"It's a pretty picture, Adele, but it's your men I need to look at. I'm not signing with a pack of tenderfeet and get myself killed. Have all six in a poker game tonight at the Star and I'll look them over, then I'll tell you."

She moved up close to him. "And right now?"

He leaned in and kissed her forehead. "Right now, Adele, I have to go meet the stage."

"What?"

"A letter, a very important letter about my friend Abigail from California, who is expected in town any day now."

Adele's pout deepened, then she wrinkled her forehead. At last a thin smile broke through. "Well, all right, but after we're working together. . . ."

Jim picked up his hat and went to the door. She hadn't bothered to cover herself.

He grinned at her once more and went out into the bright afternoon sunshine.

CHAPTER FIVE

Ed Percival looked like almost anything but what he was, the owner of Bisbee's biggest, wildest, womanest saloon. The Star and Garter had been just another place to guzzle booze until Ed took it over five years before. Since then he'd boosted it to the top of the stack.

He was short, chunky, with a fat, round face that was a constant shade of pink no matter how little or how much sunshine he absorbed. His cheeks puffed out giving him a roly-poly look of the perpetual clown. But if you looked closer at his eyes, you saw a deep brown shade of finely sanded and polished hickory wood. Nothing of importance got past his eyes, all noted and recorded in the most fantastic mind in the West. Men said he could remember the names and addresses of everyone he had ever known, both here and in Philadelphia, where he came from originally. With faces he was as good, pinning the exact name to the right face even if he hadn't seen you for ten years.

He tended to wear clothes a little too fancy for the occasion, since he had been brought up in the very polite society of the Pennsylvania city. He never ate dinner until he was properly dressed for it; always wore a white shirt and tie under his fifty dollar suits. He was judged a "dandy" at first glance but quickly won the respect and envy of every businessman in town for the quick and sure way he took the staggering saloon and turned it into a gold mine.

His costume was never complete unless he had his walking stick, one specially made shorter to adjust to his five-feet and four-inch height. It was silver tipped on the bottom and the head of it had a fancy gold crown with the seal of his family engraved on it.

Ed Percival leaned back in the leather chair and wiped his hands on the linen napkin. His eyes darted toward the waitress from the hotel, who had brought his noon meal from the kitchen in a special basket so it wouldn't cool down.

"Janice, isn't it? Yes, Janice Muldrow. You may give my compliments to the chef, Janice. The meal was excellent, only remind him that my potatoes *always* must be baked in the skins, *then* removed, seasoned, mixed with the cheese sauce and repacked in the shell." He smiled and flipped her a silver dollar tip. "That will be all, Janice."

She almost forgot and bowed, then she curtsied quickly so he wouldn't see how clumsy she was doing it, picked up the tray and basket and hurried out the door.

Ed watched her go with a small frown. They would never learn. It had taken him six months to find a decent cook in this part of the country, and at last he had to go to San Francisco and bring one back. Now the clown was trying to cut corners already. Ed snipped off the end of a cigar and lighted it with a sulphur match he tore off a round cluster. The cowboys in his saloon called them "stinkers" and from the strong sulphur smell he knew why.

The man stood, and with the rolling gait so common to short, fat men, moved to the window. The curtains had come from San Francisco too, and his desk and the two chairs. They had cost him a small fortune, but a few civilized comforts made up for this outlandish country.

He took a long pull on the cigar, blew two perfect smoke rings and waited until they floated to the ceiling. But this was the place he had chosen to make his fortune and he was well on his way. He had laughed when they told him the Territory of Arizona permitted wide-open gambling and prostitution — as long as the place was well run, clean and there were not more than two fights a night or one killing a week.

He had been on the first stage west and after a week's torture on the rock-hard seat of the devil's own invention, he had landed in Bisbee with a thousand dollars in gold in his moneybelt and a hankering for some action.

A figure striding across the street interrupted his thoughts. It was Jim Steel, a man Ed had tangled with once before, three years ago when his standing in the community wasn't as solid as it was today. He frowned, letting the thick brown brows hood his eyes. Something had to be done about that man, but the critical question was when? He had watched Jim closely since he came back to town. For a while Ed thought Jim had been drawn to the scent of gold, but gradually, as he watched the man side more and more with the sheriff, the idea paled.

But the man was a problem. Ed thought a moment of what hung in the balance and he shivered. The cigar smoke was heavy in the room before Ed turned away from the window. He had been visualizing how a ton of gold would look. Say it was in twenty-five pound ingots, there would be a stack of eighty such bars of gold! He was stacking them five high in his mind's eye when the knock came on the door.

"Yes?" he said and the stacks of gold vanished before his eyes. When he turned toward the door, the frown evaporated from his face and a smile slid into its place. The girl was Marybelle, his own private masseuse. She was nineteen, with soft golden hair, a fine, thin figure with big breasts. Now, she wore a bath robe covering her delightful body.

"Are you ready for your rubdown, Mr. Percival?" she asked, a note of tease in her voice.

"Ready, and you are three minutes late." He turned to the couch of black leather and sat down, letting the girl undo his tie, then his vest and his shirt. She folded them neatly on a chair placed for the purpose. He lay down on the leather after Marybelle had placed a soft towel over the couch. Her hands flew over his back delightfully. Oh, he knew it wasn't a good job like his masseur did back in Philadelphia, but the inevitable outcome was so much more satisfying.

As her hands worked on him he tried to think about Jim Steel. He would make some inquiries, find out more about him. The girl, Adele, had been a regular with him three years ago. She would find out anything she could for him. A soft glow spread over him as the half bottle of wine he had for lunch took effect. He rolled over on his back and watched the girl. A thin line of perspiration had formed over her eyes as she concentrated on loosening up his tight muscles. Ed looked down, saw the robe had fallen open and the swaying of her full breasts delighted him. Ed Percival licked his lips and pulled the young girl toward him.

It was more than an hour later before Marybelle put on the robe and slipped out of the room, the ten dollar gold piece held tightly in her hand.

Ed had bathed in his adjoining bath room, dressed and was sitting at his desk waiting when Red Paulson came into the room without knocking.

"Don't you ever knock, you lout?"

Red never broke stride, swung the door so it slammed and sat down in the hand-carved cherrywood chair beside the desk.

"Hell, Ed, I only knock on whore's doors." He laughed, howling at his own humor. Ed's mouth twitched once but that was the only reaction.

"What do you know about this new man, Steel?"

"Well, now, Ed. 'Pears you know him as well as I do. Boys say you tangled with him over staying open too late, and you lost. Trial and everything. I knew him from back six, seven years ago. Little fracas up in Kansas, I think. Don't get your horse in a sweat over him. Hell, he ain't even a lawman no more."

"You mean on the outside. Maybe he's a Texas Ranger, or something."

"We're in Arizona, Ed. No Texas Rangers around here. Got no authority."

"What about a U.S. Marshal, he'd have the power."

Red rubbed his shaved head with his hand, a curious look on his face. "Hey, you got something on the hook? You got maybe a prison record, or you wanted by the U.S. Marshals?"

"No, no, of course not. Preposterous." He stood and walked to the window, then back. "I just don't want anything to go wrong. And he could be a marshal. They don't show badges, not until they make an arrest."

"Okay, stop blowing like a piebald pony. I'll check it out again, but I tell you he's no marshal and no deputy marshal. I can smell law a mile away."

"You do that, Mr. Paulson. And be sure you are correct. You know I don't allow for any mistakes."

"Yeah."

"You mentioned something about another job."

"Just keep watching for that wagon. And no more slaughter jobs. That last work of yours could have a regiment of cavalry on our backs, just when we don't want them."

"We had to check it out, and their damn guards were too good for my boys to get through at night."

"So you shoot them all, murder twelve men, and then ride off like you're going to some picnic."

"All right, I said I wouldn't do it again."

Ed raised the heavy walking stick and aimed it at the man with the red beard.

"Just be sure you don't. Now, we decided we should eliminate the sheriff before the wagon gets here. But not too quickly. Have your scouts seen anything yet?"

"Nothing. Got men a day's ride west, northwest and due north, and they ain't seen anything that even looks like a wagon for two days."

"Just be sure to check out *every* wagon.

We don't know if it will be mixed in with a batch of ex-pioneers going back East, or in an army train, or just a lone wandering wagon of some freight outfit."

"Don't worry, my boys know how to do that."

"They better. Soon as you see the right wagon we take care of the sheriff. What about Jim Steel? Is he dangerous? Should we plan something special for him as well?"

"Be a personal pleasure. Give my left leg to gun him down. No extra charge!"

"Mr. Paulson, don't be so impetuous. All in good time." Ed changed his mood, took a long pull on the cigar and blew out the smoke. "Have you been enjoying yourself these nights, Mr. Paulson?"

Red laughed, a deep, dirty, belly-laugh that rolled up and out of his throat like a torrent. "Yeah, Ed, I been enjoying. Hell, have I been having a time. Been picking a new one each night, see, and I'm going right through your stable. When I get done, I think I'll try two at once."

"I had a less vulgar reason behind my question. You see, this is just the start. I intend to have Star and Garter saloons all over the state. In every city where there's a need for a saloon, the Star and Garter will move in. With this money we get from the gold wagon, we'll be able to open five or six at a time. I'll need a man to move around and set them up, get the fancy women lined up, get in the tables, *you know.*"

"You want me to work for you full time."

"Yes, it had occurred to me."

"Well, a regular dandy, me?"

"You'll need a bit of polishing, some good clothes, some training about manners and diplomacy, but I think you might work out very well."

"But first, we get the gold, right?"

"Right, Mr. Paulson, first we get the gold." He put his feet up on a stool and blew out cigar smoke. "The gold, and then Bisbee is in my pocket. I'll buy out the other saloons and run them too, to keep out competition. Then I'll buy the hotel, the general store and the freight lines and I'll have this town by the scruff of its neck. Anything I say will go. I'll bring in my own sheriff, get him elected legal and proper. Then I won't have to worry about the territorial boys. They won't sniff down here, long as I keep everything running smooth and easy. By the time I get my saloons all over the state I'll start working toward the capitol. Mr. Paulson, I could be the territorial governor some day!"

Red grinned. He had this one under his thumb. Now if he could get him drunk.

"Hey, Ed, still got that bottle of good whiskey in your desk? How about a little snort to celebrate with?"

Ed reached for the drawer, nodding. He came up with the strange square bottle Red had seen before and poured two small glasses full.

Ed sipped his, Red threw half of it down his throat and welcomed the burning sensation. He wheezed once and reached for the bottle. "Let me tell you, Ed, how I plan to take care of this no-count sheriff when the time comes."

Outside the Star and across the street, Jim Steel had stopped, not sure where to go next. He had been heading for the sheriff's office automatically. He had fallen into the old habit easily. Too easily. He glanced up at the second floor front window over the Star. That was where Ed Percival had his office. Spiffed up like a fancy woman's parlor. Jim turned to the hotel. He needed a good night's sleep and it wouldn't hurt to start on it right now.

He had just moved across the dusty street to the boards on the other side when he heard the horses. He waited. A moment later a dozen blue-shirts came pounding around the corner of Main Street. They were followed by another twelve of the pony soldiers. The troop slowed to a walk through the rest of town and the officer at the lead pulled in at the sheriff's office. He spoke quietly to a sergeant at his side who turned and took charge of the men.

As the officer swung down slowly from the saddle, Jim reversed his direction and got to the door of the sheriff's office at the same time the young officer did. Jim held the door for him, wondering how it would feel to be so close to a Yankee uniform again, especially an officer. It hadn't changed much. Jim sensed an aloofness, a coldness about the man and knew that he had tightened up when the officer had looked at him. He never had been able to relax when the officer people were around.

He went into the office behind the man and watched the soldier and lawman shake hands.

"Sit down, Lieutenant, sit down and rest yourself. Coffee?" Luke poured a cup and handed it to the soldier, then pushed in behind the desk and rubbed his face.

"Lieutenant, I'd guess you're hunting an army wagon and twelve men who should have been reporting in to your people at the fort."

"Yes, sir. That's right, but how did you know?"

"Your patrol and its wagon were ambushed about four miles east of here yesterday afternoon. Jim and I checked it out this morning and brought back what we could salvage of the wagon and one rifle."

The soldier looked like he had been kicked in the stomach. He tried to talk several times. When the words came out they were tortured. "All twelve of them, dead?"

"Yes. We buried them this morning. The ambush came from both sides of a small canyon. I made some sketches of it."

Luke took out his paper and handed it to the officer. He looked at it, and shook his head. "I had some good friends on that patrol." He scanned the paper again. "All right if I keep this?" Luke nodded. "Would you date it and sign it for me, sir?"

Luke did the chore painfully with his twisted fingers.

The officer stood up. "Sheriff, we'll camp here and wait for further orders. Is there some place with water where we can set up camp outside town?"

Luke told him about the cottonwoods, half a mile back on the trail they had come in. They went outside and Jim watched the sergeant get the order from the officer. He picked out two men and by the time they were ready, the young lieutenant had a dispatch case ready for them. He sealed it and handed it to the older man. The two took off down Main Street at a trot. Jim was glad he wasn't the one taking the sad news back to the fort.

CHAPTER SIX

As Jim watched the army turn around and move out toward the cottonwoods, he remembered the letter. The hoped-for letter. He went to the stage and freighting office where the small post office functioned in one end of the building.

The clerk knew him from before and sorted through the general delivery stack of mail quickly, coming up with one long envelope for Jim. He took it with him outside and sat in the sun along the side of the unpainted wooden building as he read it.

"Dear Jim. Abigail and her locket are still on the way. Right up to the last minute I was supposed to go along to keep Abigail company, but they decided I should stay here. I was disappointed, but know that you'll be able to take care of Aunt Abigail for us. Remember she is honored and treasured highly by all of us here. We think it would be best for her if you did not plan on a large celebration for her. Just something intimate yet meaningful to let her know we all appreciate what she has done and will do for all of us.

"The stage was several days late here, and we have heard that heavy rains and some land-slides have meant further delay, so our time schedule is simply not workable any more. Some of the rivers have been giving trouble along the way, but we pray the rains won't continue.

"Let us know by letter how everything goes and when you'll be returning here with Abigail. Sorry I couldn't come all the way, but you know how crotchety these older people become sometimes. She simply ordered me off the wagon and there was nothing I could do about it."

Jim was grinning as he finished the letter. That Dan Barton was quite a guy. What an imagination. But from that coded letter Jim worked out several obvious messages. First was the post mark. Yuma, Arizona Territory. The gold wagon was as far as Yuma, and Barton had been put off the wagon at Yuma.

82

Why? He didn't know. But bad weather had held up the wagon. That was acceptable. No danger in it at least. But the part about a big celebration for their favorite aunt stumped him. What was Barton trying to tell him? The last time he had heard from Barton nothing had changed, one wagon and sixteen troopers, eighteen men in all. Jim had planned on finding four good men in Bisbee. Now he didn't know what to do.

Jim glanced at the position of the sun. Ever since he could remember, he could tell what time it was by the position of the big star in the sky. Nearly four o'clock. Some men he knew wore watches. A cowboy wouldn't be caught near one of the contraptions. The other hands would call him a Waterbury man and he would have trouble shaking the monicker on that range. As more and more of his life became regulated by a clock, Jim knew he would have to come to it eventually. At least he would have sense enough to hide the blamed thing in his pocket!

Too early for supper, and the hotshot crew Adele had been paying to sit on their saddles wouldn't be at the Star until after six. Jim knew what he wanted to do, what he should do — go over and apologize to Kathy for flying off his pitchfork handle when she asked about his being a deputy. He wanted to, but that wide, thick streak of stubborn in him wouldn't give way.

He folded the letter carefully, putting it in his pants pocket beside the telegram, then tore the envelope into a dozen pieces and pushed dirt over them. He sat where he was, his backside in the dirt, his back pressed against the unpainted side of the stage house, letting the warm sun soak into his bones. The denim jacket he wore picked up the heat from the boards and before he knew it, he had dropped off to sleep. A cramp in his leg woke him a half hour later. He eyed the sun and thought for a few minutes about the letter. There was something in it he hadn't caught, some hidden meaning that was too hidden. He worried it some more, then pushed up from the ground and headed for the livery stable. He should have checked on the buckskin before now, but he was sure that old Ned would take care of the horses just back from a posse the way he used to.

The buckskin was in the second stall next to the door, right beside the sheriff's big gray. Both had been walked out and wiped down after the morning workout. The livery man was not in sight, so Jim found a curry comb and worked over the hide of the former outlaw pony. He threw up his head, eyed Jim from huge wall-eyes and went back to munching the dry alfalfa hay.

Jim spent the next hour checking over and filling up his small war bag and the saddle bags that made up his traveling gear. A double blanket, rolled and looped behind the saddle, completed his gear. In the saddle bags went jerky, hard biscuits, a few cans of beans and two small jars of honey. He could live for a week on those two jars of honey, and had done so more than once. There was other food, and before a trip he would add bacon, coffee and sugar, but at least he was ready in case he had to ride out in a rush.

When he was finished, he went to the little cafe where he had met Adele, and ate. There wasn't a menu. You sat down at a small table or a spot along the counter and they brought food. When you were satisfied you got up and paid them twenty-five cents at the door. Jim paid and stepped into the late evening sunshine. It was cooler now, and with his belly full he had two reasons to get on with his business. He still wasn't used to the fancy airs some of the hotels were taking on. He'd seen a western hotel in Arizona Territory that charged a dollar and a half for a meal. Course it took you over an hour to eat it; still, that was a pure waste of good money.

He thought of the gold. The time to live high hadn't come yet. But if he had that ton of gold in his pocket, then he'd begin to forget about where his next double eagle was coming from.

By the time he had this bit of range-land philosophy digested, he had moved to the front of the Star and Garter. Things were quiet. Four of the dance hall girls sat at a back table, eating what the cook called food. It came with the job and they ate it three times a day to save what little they earned.

Red Paulson didn't seem to be around yet. Jim looked at the poker tables and saw six men seated at the biggest one. Adele hovered over them like a mother hen. Jim looked through the front window at the six men and he wanted to laugh.

These were the hard, trained, desperate men Adele wanted him to lead on a gold wagon raid? Pushing through the bat-wings, he eyed them closer as he walked toward the motley group. One was little more than a boy who hadn't begun shaving yet. The next one around the table was in his sixties, with an unkempt beard and long, matted hair. The third man looked half-way decent. He was in his thirties, wore range clothes and had the sun-seared skin of a working cowboy. He constantly squinted at the cards, as if he were still on the range under the Arizona sun.

Jim wrote off the last three as saddle bums looking for an easy dollar, which could be good or bad depending on the kind of men under the clothes.

Jim walked up to the table and tapped the kid on the shoulder. The boy turned.

"On your feet!" Jim snapped.

When the boy stood up nervously, Jim pushed him to one side and sat down. "I want to play some poker and this looks like the only game in town."

They started a new hand. No one said a word. He played close and won the first game with a pair of queens. None of the men were poker players. One thought he was. On the next hand Jim bluffed the table with a king-high hand and won a pot of almost ten dollars.

He stood up and dropped the deck. "I can't waste my time here, any objections?" Nobody said a word, but as he stood, the cowboy across the table rose too.

"Nobody quits when he's ahead in this game."

"Who says?"

"Me, Duke Jannis."

Duke moved quickly and stood in front of Jim by the time he had his chair pushed in. Jim's hands were at his side. His face had softened, he seemed entirely relaxed. Suddenly his fist shot upward, slashing across Duke's chin, staggering him. Jim was all business now, digging his left hand into Duke's stomach and as he bent over bringing another uppercut to the man's jaw. Duke's eyes went wide and he crumpled on the floor, groaning.

Jim pushed the money he had won back into the center of the table. "I didn't come here for your money." He turned, put his arm around Adele and walked her to the bar.

"Are you out of your mind?" he said quietly to the woman. "I wouldn't go to an alley-cat fight with that bunch. Duke is the only one with any guts. You can stick the rest of them in your ear. Get five more like Duke and you got yourself a partner."

"Partner?" she asked.

"Right, fifty, fifty. Half for me, and half for you and the boys." He grinned at her surprise. "Take it or forget it, baby. I know a hell of a lot more about that wagon than you do. I've got another partner riding on board."

Jim turned and walked out of the Star. He

didn't want too many people to see him talking to Adele and get curious.

As he hit the boardwalk he turned, found a chair in front of the general store and sat a moment. The owner was carrying tools and horse collars back inside, getting ready to close up. He came to a big wooden box and started to tug at it, then looked over at Jim. Jim knew the glance was coming and had his eyes staring in the opposite direction. He wanted to chuckle, but decided against it. That was something he had to fight, that wanting to help people. He had to think about himself, worry about his own hide and be ready to grab that gold when the time came.

Just before McGaffery closed up his store, Jim walked inside. He went to the big wooden box filled with three-foot long chunks of winter ice and straw and found a slab of bacon he liked. He slammed the lid, then remembered he needed coffee. At the counter he saw a basket of fresh apples and put six of them on his stack of supplies.

"How much?" he asked McCaffery, the little store owner.

McCaffery paused and wiped a drip of sweat off his nose.

"Well now, I guess you can wait a minute while I get this stack of goods out of the weather, can't ye? 'Pears like you've changed good deal since you did some law work for us, Jim."

" 'Pears so, McCaffery. I don't let people walk all over me any more. You want cash money for this stack or do I walk out with it like Red Paulson does?"

McCaffery snorted and went behind the counter, wrapping the slab of bacon in white paper and moving the pile over as he figured the bill. "Sixty-one cents," he said. "You still eat heavy, I see." There was the start of a sparkle in the older man's eyes now. Jim had always liked the merchant when he had been here before. He paid for the goods, put the apples in his pockets and carried the rest in his hands to the livery.

Old Ned had just finished cleaning the stalls. He grinned up at Jim with the stumps of his teeth showing brown and crooked. He spat a stream of tobacco juice into a stall.

"Dogged if it ain't Jim. Hi there, Sheriff."

"I'm not the sheriff anymore, Ned, you remember. I've been gone two years."

"That long? Dogged if it don't seem like day before last week." He shook his head. "Well, dogged if it ain't good to have you back. Staying long?"

"Doubt it, Ned. Right now I need my

horse. He get some oats?"

"All he wanted, and some of that new alfalfa."

Jim threw a saddle blanket over the buckskin and began to saddle up. He tightened the cinch strap and saw it was two holes shy of normal. His fist walloped into the side of the big horse, who promptly let out a massive burst of air through his mouth, then Jim cinched the strap properly.

When he was finished saddling he paid his tab with the stable man.

"Dogged, you're coming back, ain't ya?"

Jim reset his hat and laughed. "Be very mad if I don't make it back, Ned. Now you take care of things." He mounted and rode out of the stable barn, walking the buckskin past the hotel and on toward Luke Tabor's sheriff's house.

Kathy was just coming back with Luke's dinner basket. Jim tied up the horse at the gate and held it open for her.

"Busy?"

"No, Jim. I'm glad you stopped by. Come on in and help me do the dishes."

He grinned. She knew he hated to wash dishes. It was her way of saying all was forgiven. As soon as the kitchen door had closed behind them, Kathy reached up and kissed his lips, lingering there and putting her arms around him.

She came away from his lips and nestled her head under his chin.

"Oh, Jim, you don't know how much I've dreamed of kissing you that way, a real woman's kiss. Sometimes a woman knows things a man can't. I mean, right now I know you're my man. And I knew it three years ago, a month before you left. It's my woman's intuition, whatever that is. But somehow I know that you and I were supposed to go through life together."

Jim pulled up her chin and kissed her, hard and demanding, then gently pushed her away.

"Kathy, what put ideas like those in that pretty little head of yours? You don't know what it means to be a woman, to love a man."

Her eyes shot sparks at him. "No, but I've had chances. I wanted to wait for you. Was that my first mistake?"

"Easy now. Don't go rearing like a wild filly. I meant you've got lots of time."

She put her arms around him again, pushing her body hard against his. "Jim, you come back after three years, and we get into a fight and you get mad and leave, and I don't know if you'll be back for three years again. I *haven't* got lots of time. I'll be an old maid soon. Darling, I'm so in love with you that I don't know what I'll do. I just can't stand it."

"Now you sound like the way the fancy women talk."

She slapped him, then kissed his cheek. Her eyes turned suspicious. "How do you know how the loose, immoral women in the dance halls talk?"

"I've heard."

"Have you ever made love to them?"

Jim laughed. "That's no question for you to ask."

"Why not? I'm a big girl. I know about the girls and boys, the birds and the bees."

"Why do you want to know?"

She reddened. "Well, darling, if that's part of loving you and taking care of you, then I want to be able to do that too."

Jim kissed her cheek and led her by the hand into the kitchen where he began unpacking the basket of dishes.

"Don't worry, when that time comes you won't have any trouble taking care of your man. Now hush up this kind of talk and do the dishes while I watch."

She frowned at him and stamped her foot once, but she saw he had sat down backwards on a chair, leaning against the back of it. She sighed, then turned to the dishes.

"Looks like you're ready to ride," she said, a tightness coming into her voice.

"Just a couple of days."

"And people will be shooting at you?"

Jim laughed. "I hope not. I'm just going on a nice quiet ride and look at the country."

"I hope so!" There was a catch in her voice. "Right now I hate that horse of yours! I hate stages and trains and wagons and anything that takes you away from me!"

Jim felt his blood racing. He wanted to make love to her right now, but you don't love a girl like Kathy and walk away. The time to walk was right now — fast. He caught her shoulders, kissed her warm lips lightly, then pushed her away.

"I've got to go, but I'll be back. Tell Luke I'll be back in two days and give him some help. This is a job I've got to do."

As he watched her eyes he saw the anger and the fright surge into them. He bent and kissed her lips again, harder now, longer. Her arms came around him and she sighed.

It took all of his will power to ease away from her. "I'll be back and it won't be three years!"

He ran to the door and went out it without looking back. If he had looked, he was sure he would have gone back to her right then.

He closed the front gate quietly, took the

reins of the buckskin and walked him slowly out of town. He headed to the south, just in case anyone was watching. Once he cleared the last house he went another half mile, then made a wide arc to the west and settled down on the little stage road that led toward Miller peak and eventually northwest, aiming for Tucson. It would be a rugged two or three days, but he had to check on all possible routes to see if any wagon traffic was moving.

CHAPTER SEVEN

The first night out he rode until the stars showed him it was past midnight. He had covered most of the distance toward Miller peak, turned north, following the stage road, and met no one. He saw one wagon camped to the side of the trail. He had crawled up on foot to survey the party. It was a rancher heading for Bisbee for supplies. He was old, shaggy, with the look of a prospector turned rancher.

Jim didn't bother making himself known, just walked back to his horse and rode another hour before he found a swatch of brush beside a wash where he tied up Hamlet, his horse, and stretched out on his blankets.

He hadn't thought about the name of his horse for a long time. He picked up the nag in Kansas almost two years back from a traveling show. The horses all had Shakespearean characters' names. Hamlet got too frisky for the performances and had to go. Hamlet. Jim got the book once and tried to read it, but he couldn't understand the story. He did remember the line about something being rotten in Denmark. That's what he was thinking about as he went to sleep.

He was up before the sun, frying bacon over a small, smokeless cooking fire, and brewing up his coffee. The bacon on the hard biscuits made a solid breakfast. A half hour after he woke he was in the saddle moving north. He left the trail now and cut across country working toward a high point where he remembered he could see both the main trails from Tucson.

By noon he had seen only one small band of Indians on a hunting trip, two horsemen riding north and a small smoke smudge off any of the trails he knew. He would investigate the smoke on his way back to town. He pushed on, overtaking three covered wagons heading west, but giving them a wide berth so they didn't even know he was around. The country became dryer and flattened out so he could see for ten miles before the haze and the dust from a brisk wind clouded the distance.

He used his water sparingly now, and

moved the big buckskin at the pace he wanted to travel. The desert was as hot and unforgiving as ever. Why did men want to live in this hell hole of a territory?

He longed for the fresh green of a Texas hillside, or the smooth sweep of fresh green grass on a Kansas plain. But he was here and he had a job to do, and if it came off right, he could pick and choose exactly where he wanted to live.

Jim camped that night as soon as the sun went down. He was as close to Tucson as he wanted to go. He had passed several ranches, some of them new to him, and he wondered how they scratched a living out of the sand and rocks. Most were situated in small valleys; two had set up a series of windmills to try to irrigate the bottomland to grow alfalfa and native grass for hay for the steers. Jim had been startled by the sudden green square appearing in the desert in front of him and had worked his way close enough to the outfit to find out what they were doing.

But he saw no gold wagon.

He saw nothing that even looked like one wagon carrying a ton of gold.

His camp was against a limestone cliff that had a small overhang of granite. Hamlet munched on some dry grass and had a belly-full of water from the last spring, which they had found right where it was supposed to be.

Jim lay back on his blankets watching the sudden cloud drift past the moon. He had eaten only twice that day, and could feel his stomach start to tighten now. It couldn't shrink much in two or three days, he knew, but the familiar grinding deep in his gut brought back memories of the war, when they went without any food for three and four days during one bad spell.

But he didn't want to think of the war. He'd rather think of the ton of gold, and of the soft, gentle body of Kathy and her beautiful face and hair. He was still thinking about her as he went to sleep, and sometime before morning he dreamed of her.

He woke up before dawn, stiff and cold in the desert half-light. Over a small fire he fried ten thick slices of bacon and ate them along with a can of beans and the rest of the hard biscuits. He put jerky in his shirt pocket to chew on during the day's ride.

Before he left the spot, he took a long look at the country he could see from the ledge. Nothing moving, not even a hawk. He would swing back cross country toward Tombstone and check the north trail. It was rugged riding. One time he thought he saw someone ahead of him. He stopped for half an hour checking the down grade in front of him, but again, nothing moved, not even a rattlesnake. He worked slowly down the ravine ahead, then on a hunch angled through a smattering of pine and oak up the side of the gully until he reached the ridgeline and worked along it. It was slow going, and twice he had to get off and lead the buckskin through rocks. The pines concealed him here, but also made his movement slower.

When he had worked to the place he wanted, he tied Hamlet, and moved silently toward the cliff that dropped away sharply into the small valley below. He saw the two horses at once, tied behind huge slabs of rock that had thundered from the cliff ages ago. Jim wiped his eyes and checked again. The safest trail led directly down the watercourse, where some sand and dirt and a little grass had sprouted. Half way down the ravine he spotted the men, lying behind rocks, one on each side of the trail. Both had rifles laid out and pistols.

He was too far away to recognize the men. The horses were easier — one a light gray, the other a red. Jim wondered how long the men would wait. He had been careless letting them spot him. Now he would be more careful. He turned the buckskin over the ridge and worked his way down the other side. When he came out of the ravine into the open desert, he let Hamlet out for a good run, pulled him down after a quarter of a mile and let him blow. With any luck at all they both would be back in Bisbee before sundown.

Jim used his war training now, checking each new area he went into, using the cover that was available, working through water courses, draws, staying off ridgelines, and utilizing any trees or brush he could find. As he worked his way toward the Tombstone road he felt a sudden chill, as if someone had a rifle sighted on his back. He turned quickly but there was nothing behind him but rocks, sand and a buzzard high overhead.

He rode a little faster then. Hamlet was holding up well — he'd had an easy morning — but now Jim called on him for more speed and he complained, with a toss of his head. But they moved ahead steadily.

Near noon he spotted a big dust on the Tombstone trail and pulled ahead of it to check. As he did, the wagons stopped and quick cooking fires were built. They were homesteaders; each of the four wagons had a walking plow tied to the side.

Jim rode quickly down to the wagons, hailed the first man he saw and was invited in to eat. It was a community kitchen arrangement.

The leader of the band was a grizzled, bearded man of about sixty, but hard as a rod. He squinted at Jim, scowled at the rifle in his boot and the six gun at his hip.

"Jed," the old man said, holding out his hand. "Jed Smith, this is my family and we're moving west."

"Jim," he said, taking the firm hand. "And looks like I'm heading the wrong direction."

"Freedom, that's what we're looking for. Where a man can worship the way he wants to."

"Thought a man could do that most anywhere."

Jed looked up as he handed Jim a big tin plate. "Lots of us thought the same thing in Missouri and in Illinois and in New York." He paused motioning Jim up to the serving kettle. "Now we're going to the Land of Zion, to Salt Lake City."

Jim nodded, held his plate as a stout, red-faced woman dished out two dippers-full of stew, floating with carrots and potatoes and chunks of meat. The next woman put a slab of cornbread on his plate and the third woman gave him a steaming cup of coffee. He was amazed the meal had been heated up so quickly.

He sat down beside Jed Smith and looked at the line at the food place. He saw only the three grown women and eighteen or twenty youngsters, from toddlers to teenagers, standing quietly in line. That was when he remembered, Salt Lake City was a Mormon settlement. And the Mormons could have as many wives as they could provide for. Looked like Jed Smith was a good provider.

He talked with Jed, telling him some of the troubles he would find on the trail north to Tucson and then to Phoenix. He suggested they head on north to Flagstaff before going west into Nevada. But as he talked, his mind was never far from the gold wagon. He was thinking what a perfect camouflage a family group would be for the gold shipment. Who would suspect two men and their families heading back east by wagon. The gold could be split between the two. . . . No, Barton said there was only one wagon now. He'd be suspicious of every wagon he saw. The army must have a plan of changing the route and the disguise of the actual gold wagon every few hundred miles.

When the food was cleaned off the plates, an eager-faced little boy picked them up and put them in a pot of steaming soapy water where another lad washed them. Less than half an hour after the party stopped, they were back in the wagons and moving out. Jim waved a final goodbye and left the group, moving off the trail and into the rougher country, where he could see the stage-road but not be seen from it.

The closer he came to Bisbee, the more sure he was that the real gold wagon would come in from the west, and the more he thought about it the firmer his belief was that it would come with stealth or with surprise, but definitely not with an armored troop of protectors. So every wagon was suspect, big or little, protected or alone.

He circled Bisbee again, coming in from the south — the same direction he had left town from, in case anyone was interested. He went straight to the livery stable and asked Ned to rub down the buckskin.

"You ain't heard yet about Luke Tabor?"

Jim looked up quickly. "No."

"Got himself shot up and stomped some, he. . . ."

Jim didn't wait to hear the rest. He was running hard down the street, changing it to a steady jog as he covered the ground to the sheriff's house as fast as he could. He knocked on the front door, then turned the knob and went inside. Kathy had just come from the bedroom to answer the knock. Her face was drawn and tired, and when she saw him angry wrinkles showed around her eyes.

"Why did you leave him just when he needed you the most?" Her eyes were sad as well as angry. He touched her shoulder and went past her into the big bedroom. Luke lay under the sheet, his left arm bound tightly against a board where the doctor had tied it. Luke's face had a dozen bruises, and one eye was swollen shut. His other eye was bandaged. One side of his mouth hung down where it had been torn.

"That you, Jim?" Luke said.

Jim frowned as he heard the voice, it was that of an old man, one ready to give up and forget ambition, justice, and right from wrong, and turn it all over to somebody else.

"Yeah, Luke, I'm back. Sorry I wasn't here. Who did it?"

"Can't be sure, Jim. Too dark."

Kathy touched his sleeve, motioning him out.

"Luke, I'll be right here, now don't worry. I'll take care of things. You get some sleep."

As he went out the door, Kathy closed it gently behind him and he could see she had been crying. He reached for her and she came to him like a hurt puppy. When she had let some of the anger and frustration drain out of her with the tears, she pushed away and sat down at the kitchen table, pointing to the other chair.

He sat. "Tell me what happened and who did it."

"Red Paulson. That's who Dad thinks it was, and the talk around town is the same. It happened the same night you left. Dad was making his rounds — checking the saloons and seeing that doors were locked — when somebody hit him from behind and pulled him into the alley by the general store. No lights around there at all. One man held Dad while another one hit him. When he couldn't stand up any more they kicked him. Then before they left they shot him in both arms. They tried to break his arms. The left one did break in the elbow. Doc said it probably will heal stiff. On his right one the bullet just missed the bone.

"As soon as they shot him, the men ran down the alley and were gone before somebody found him and ran for Doc."

"Jail locked?" Jim asked. His eyes were cold and deadly. He hadn't felt this way in a long time. The girl gave him the ring of keys and he went out the door without

106

another word. He swore he'd never wear a badge again, but this was different. He walked quickly, the frigid rage building with every step until he had trouble opening the jail door. Inside he lit a lamp, so it would be burning when he came back, and found the deputy badge in the drawer. After pinning it on his denim shirt he unlocked the chain around the rifles and shotguns, took out a new Greener double barrel and loaded it. He pocketed two more of the shells, noting with satisfaction they were loaded with eight chunks of lead. He wondered what kind of pattern the slugs would make at twenty feet. Jim relocked the padlock on the guns and went to the door. His six gun was loaded and ready, and so was he.

The first place he looked was the Star. Ed Percival seemed ready for him when he came in. He looked at the deputy badge and smiled.

"Evening, Deputy, what can we do for you tonight?"

"I'm skunk hunting, is he here?"

"Whatever do you mean?"

"You know damn well *what* and *who* I mean," Jim said taking a long step forward, catching Percival by his fancy shirt and tie and lifting him off the floor with one hand. "You tell that back-stabbing rattlesnake of

107

yours that I'll get him. It won't do him no good to run. I can run as fast and as far as he can. He better not use his real name anymore, because every sheriff and marshal in the country is going to have a wanted poster on him just as soon as I can get them printed up and mailed."

He dropped the little man who had been flailing his arms trying to keep his balance.

"I assure you sir, that. . . ."

Jim hit him with the side of his hand, but the blow had all the hate and frustration in it Jim had stored up in the last half hour. Ed Percival was slammed to one side, stumbled, fell and skidded three feet on the polished floor.

Jim didn't wait to watch him stop skidding. He whirled and marched to the door, where he turned and yelled at the crowd.

"Anybody knows where that back-shooting Red Paulson is can tell him for me that the only way he'll get me off his neck is to kill me. And he better make his play before I find him and make mine."

He blasted through the bat-wings in a rage that left him curiously weak. A moment later he walked down the boardwalk and changed into a different man. He was a target now, and he knew it. He slid from one post to the next, and ran across the street hoping Red Paulson wasn't in Percival's office with a Remington waiting for him. But nothing happened. Inside the sheriff's office he turned down the light and wrote a note which he had delivered to Adele.

An hour later Adele knocked on the back door of the jail and he let her into the store room. There was no light at all.

"Did Paulson do it?"

"Yes, Jim. As near as I can tell. I saw him come in that night and get some whiskey to pour over his knuckles. He was a little drunk and laughing a lot. I saw him reload two shells in his six gun and then he went up to talk to Percival.

"Usually Ed don't talk business at night. He sits up there and reads and writes poetry, while we do the work."

"But Red went up and got in?"

"Yes and stayed an hour. When he came down he was passing out silver dollar tips like they were candy. That night he took two of the girls to a special room upstairs."

"A little extra payoff?"

"Seemed that way. He's never been let in that room before."

"Where is he now?"

"I don't know. Haven't seen him since that night. He's got some more men now, might be camping out with them."

Jim thought about it. "He isn't north, I just came through there, and there's no water south or east. He must be west."

"Waiting for the gold wagon?" she asked.

"Yes, and waiting for me to let down my guard. If they took Luke out of the play, I have to be next. That means I have to go coyote hunting. And I have to go out tonight!"

CHAPTER EIGHT

Jim let Adele out the back door without showing a light, hoping no one noticed her coming up the alley. He had to get a different horse and have Ned saddle him. He should restock his saddle bags, but there wouldn't be time for that. He locked the front door and ran out the back to find Ned currying his pet filly.

Ned went to work getting the sheriff's horse ready, saying Luke wouldn't mind. Jim promised to be back in half an hour — ready to go.

He walked quickly back to the jail, unlocked the rear door and took the key inside with him. He checked the cupboard where he used to keep emergency rations. There were two cans of beans, half a dozen chocolate bars, a can of coffee and a jar of honey. He was hungry, but should he stop at the cafe or eat something here? He decided to eat what he had and put a pot of water on the little wood stove to heat up. As it heated he sat down at the desk and looked at the wanted poster file. One of the faces looked familiar, but he couldn't tie down a name or place.

He closed his eyes and rubbed them with his hand, just for a moment. . . .

When Jim woke up, it was morning. He stretched, saw where he had pushed back papers on the desk with his arms as he had slept. He banged the desk hard with his hand and hurried over to the livery.

Ned had fallen asleep in an open stall, and he knuckled his eyes open as Jim shook him.

"That horse ready to go, Ned?" Jim asked.

"Horse, what horse? Oh, yeah, Sheriff." He squinted at the sunshine. "You shore take a long time for half an hour."

Together they unsaddled the big mare and put her in a stall. Jim threw the saddle over the hook and shook his head.

"I must have half-died last night. I'll get a breakfast and let you know what's happening."

In the cafe, as soon as he sat down a plate with four eight-inch-wide hot cakes was placed in front of him, with a dish beside it holding six strips of thick bacon. He chewed down two stacks of the flapjacks and four cups of coffee before he felt satisfied. He paid his thirty cents and went outside. Only then did he remember his warning to Red Paulson.

He didn't expect an attack in town during the day. That would be as risky for Paulson as it would for Jim to try to find his coyote camp in the sunshine. They both needed darkness for a cover.

Jim walked back to the sheriff's office, then checked with the mailman and picked up two letters for the sheriff, but nothing for him. He saw a trooper coming out of the general store and talked to him. The pony soldier didn't know a thing, only that they were still waiting orders.

Before noon a horseman reined up outside the office and stomped onto the walk, then inside. The man was a soldier and an officer.

"Morning Major," Jim said, finding a grain of satisfaction in remaining seated.

"Sheriff, you the head man?" the officer asked curtly.

"Major, let's say if you want to talk with the law in this town, you talk to me." He stood up and held out his hand. "Jim Steel, deputy. Sheriff got shot up some. What's on your mind?"

"The killers of twelve troopers. You caught

113

them yet?"

"No major, and if we did we couldn't hold them. No evidence, no witnesses, no nothing."

"I heard you were a witness, Steel. Hear you saw the whole thing while riding into town."

"That's right. You're an army man, major, not a lawyer. That's one man's word against that of eight men."

The major grimaced. "Yes, unfortunately. We've inspected the wreck and the graves, talked to Lieutenant Warbow at the cottonwoods. Now we'd like to take a look at those army wagon wheels."

Jim showed them to the major. They were behind the courthouse padlocked to a steel fence. The major noticed the bullet marks on three of them.

"All right, we'll have them picked up the next time an army wagon comes through here."

"When will that be, Major?"

"I have no way of knowing." He paused. "Oh, I and my ten men will be camping with Lt. Warbow out at the cottonwoods. If you hear anything about this Red Paulson we can use, let us know. We might take him back for military justice."

"A civilian?"

"We have a federal judge at the fort now, he could handle it quite impartially, and all very legally."

As the major turned and walked back to his horse, Jim touched the brim of his hat. "Yes sir, Major sir," he said quietly.

He kept busy until after lunch trying to figure out the system Luke had put in on complaints, arrests, and summonses. He gave up at last and had two cups of coffee for lunch. As he went back to the office after a round of the stores, he saw two pony soldiers riding through town faster than usual. They had come from the west and the closest way to the cottonwoods was right through town.

On a hunch, he saddled up Hamlet and rode quietly toward the big trees. He got there just as twenty troopers mounted up, turned into a column of twos and came toward him at a walk. The major rode at their head. He signaled a halt when Jim's horse stopped in the middle of the road facing him.

"Yes, Sheriff?"

"Saw your men come tearing through town. Just hope on the return trip you'll go slower, and not panic the population."

"I assure you, Sheriff. . . ."

"Does this mean an army wagon is coming through and we can get rid of those wheels?"

The major frowned and shook his head. "No, the wheels will remain. An army wagon is coming, but we have instructions to meet it outside of town and route it around town and to the fort in the quickest possible way. Do you have any suggestions, Sheriff?"

"No."

"In that case we'll proceed."

He motioned the troop forward and they jogged past Jim who sat and watched them go. Now what kind of double talk was that? Yes a wagon was coming, but "no" it couldn't be used to haul the wheels. The obvious answer was the wagon was already loaded to capacity.

Jim kicked the buckskin into motion, and walked him back to town. A wagon was coming, and it would have another twenty or even thirty-five more troopers as an armed escort. Was it the real one, or another dummy? Or did they decide to beef up the guard on all army rigs, to prevent the massacre that happened here near Bisbee? How could he decide if it were the real wagon? He worried it all the way back to the livery stable, then in his office. There was no way of telling how far the wagon was out, but it had to be at least a day, and it was coming from the west.

He tried to remember how the troopers were outfitted. Yes, they were field-ready, which meant they could stay on the trail for a week if they had to. If they were coming back the same day, they wouldn't have needed their packs and blanket rolls.

No rush, at least not today. Jim pushed his hat down over his eyes and leaned back in the chair, perching his feet on the edge of the battle-scarred desk and relaxed. He didn't exactly go to sleep, just resting his eyes, when someone pushed in through the front door.

"What in hell are you doing sitting there?"

Jim pushed his hat back, not knowing what to expect. What he saw was Adele, looking very businesslike in pants, blouse and short leather jacket — with a huge six gun at her hip.

"Well, ain't you heard, the damn gold wagon is two days out on the Tucson trail? Time we got to moving."

"That a fact?"

Adele stared at him, her mouth open to say something, but nothing came out. She looked around for something to throw at him.

"Well of course it's a fact! What's the matter with you, Jim? Didn't you see those two trooper scouts come riding hell-bent-for-leather through town? And then half an hour later twenty pony soldiers went the other way. What else could it mean?"

"Coffee?" Jim asked getting up to pour himself a cup. She shook her head. Jim sat on the edge of the desk sipping the hot brew.

"It could mean a lot of things, Adele. I suppose you saw Red Paulson and his army ride out of town right after the soldiers?"

"Well, no. He's already out of town. But I thought. . . ."

"Have some coffee, it isn't bad." He poured a cup and handed it to her. "You want to go up against thirty to fifty mounted, armed, professional soldiers with your six?"

"How many?"

"The major had twenty, there could be twenty more with the army wagons. That's not the kind of odds we want. And if this is the right wagon, why would the army attract so much attention to it with a half a hundred men charging around it?"

"You mean this might be another dummy?"

"Oh, it will be loaded, probably with personnel records, award citations and army data, and maybe some rifles and pistols that need to be repaired. The army has run wagons around this country for years."

As they talked there was a commotion in the street outside, as people and horses and wagons pulled to one side. Another detachment of troopers came loping through town. Jim counted. There were fifteen troopers, field equipped, and two pack horses trailing the crew.

"The odds just went up," Jim said. "You still want to go riding out of here?"

"What can we do?"

"We calm down, wait a couple of days and get a good look at the wagons. If they have the gold on them, I'll know."

"We could ambush them, like Red done," she said sounding a little frantic.

Jim marched her to the door. "Ambush fifty men? They'll be watching for that now, moving with lead scouts, with security men at each side of the column. They'll check out every possible ambush point along the way. That's probably why the army sent more men to meet this wagon, just so it doesn't get shot up."

She looked at him once more, the start of a frown on her hard face. Then she shrugged. "I guess you know best about these things, Jim. But don't try to go without me."

119

"Adele, I told you I wouldn't ride with your bunch, remember? Now why don't you go back over to the saloon and do what you know how to do." He grinned at her surprise. "And what you're damned well equipped to do."

She grinned then, winked at him and went out the door. Jim tasted the coffee, decided he'd already drunk too much and threw it out the back door. When he came back into the main part of the office, one of the barkeeps from the Star was standing nervously in the middle of the room.

"Mr. Steel?"

Jim nodded.

"Got a message for you." The barkeep handed Jim an envelope and went out the door quickly, like he was glad to get away from the jail.

Jim smiled at him, wondering at what town back down the line he'd been in trouble. It had to be somewhere, the man's hand was shaking when he handed the white envelope to Jim.

He sat down before he tore it open, ripping it across the end, blowing inside to open it up before pulling out the thin, single sheet of paper. Across the top of the paper was printed a single line: "From the desk of F. Edward Percival." Jim had a notion to

120

wad up the letter and throw it into the corner, but he didn't. He read:

"I won't talk about your argument with Red. But if you want in on something so big it will make you weak in the knees, be at the side door of the Star in five minutes. This is no trap. Red is out of town. I'm talking about almost a million dollars! Come see me and let's talk."

It was not signed. Jim folded up the note and stuffed it back in the envelope. He knew it word for word. Again his first thought was of violence, to go and gun down Percival before he could say a word, then ride out, find Red and call him out for a showdown.

But his good sense won again and he tried to think through and around it, to cover all the angles. Red was out of town. He would be checking out that wagon. So Ed must be backing him and his guns. Why did he want to see Jim? Unless he wanted two chances at the gold wagon. It had to be the wagon, nothing else in this end of the country was worth that much, not the whole town of Bisbee.

He stood and shook his head. It was no use, he wasn't even going. And it still could be a trap. He wouldn't work for Percival if he had all the gold in Washington. Just ignore him.

Jim reached for his hat. No! Go over and tell him face to face what he thought of him, and his dirty ways for picking on a crippled old man like Luke. Then knock Percival down again and remind him that not every man or every gun could be bought, no matter how much money Percival had!

Jim didn't go in the side door, nor did he go in the back way. The back was where he figured any ambush might be set up. He walked in the front door of the Star and looked at the early drinkers along the bar. The man with the apron pointed up the broad stairs near the back of the place. Jim didn't like the idea, but he went up the steps quickly and saw Percival's big front office door open. Ed stood at the door smoking a cigar.

"Jim, just the man I'm hunting for. Come in, come in."

Jim wanted to tell him then, tell him and go back down the steps, but he couldn't. He went inside and decided to wait and see what the offer was. Then he would smash it down.

Ed sat down in the big leather chair behind the desk and motioned to the other chair. Jim remained standing.

"I don't have time to dicker, Jim. I want

you on my team, not against me. You know what's happening here. Red thinks this is the right wagon."

"He thought the *last* one was the right one and killed twelve good men."

Ed shook his head. "A tragedy, nobody is more shocked and saddened than I am. But it was a risk. Now he says he's almost sure. Why else would the army use so many men? It has to be the right one."

"And you want me to raise twenty men and go help Red Paulson bushwhack fifty blue coats?"

"Well, now, Jim, nothing so tragic. But it would help to have a few more guns. We've got a surprise for the army that will stop them in their tracks. They could have a hundred troopers."

"What's the surprise?"

"After you're on my team, Jim. Then only when it happens."

"Percival, I wouldn't be on your team for all the gold in that wagon. I'd rather a desert sandstorm buried it than to let you get anywhere near it."

Percival stood up, offered Jim a cigar but had it batted out of his hands. He didn't show any anger at Jim's refusal.

"Jim, I'm a businessman. Luke was in our way and he was taken out of the way. He was a pawn and my horseman captured him in one simple move. Now I'm offering to let you into the game, to play on my side. Checkmate time is almost here and I could use an extra knight."

Jim had learned to play chess his first year as a deputy sheriff, and he knew exactly what Percival meant.

"What it all boils down to, Ed, is that you have Red Paulson leading your attack and you're not quite sure you can trust him. You want me to go along with some men and eliminate Paulson if he tries to take off with the gold."

"Exactly," Percival said.

"You can go to hell, Percival. Go straight to hell and lay on burning coals till you fry your guts out!"

Jim turned, wondering how he had kept from smashing his fists into the little man. As he turned he saw two of Percival's faro dealers standing in the doorway, each carried a sawed-off shotgun and the hammers were cocked.

CHAPTER NINE

Jim looked back at Percival who was smiling.

"You had your chance, Jim, a clean, honest chance. But some misdirected loyalty got the best of you." He came around the desk and lifted Jim's six gun from its holster, then patted his sides, chest and legs looking for other weapons.

"We can't take any chances now, Jim. It's too close. If you didn't go along with us, that made you against us, and with that badge, and all the men you know in town . . . we just couldn't permit that, could we Jim?"

Run! Jim's mind was telling him. Those aprons wouldn't shot-gun a man in the back. Run!

But a fraction of a second before the message got from his brain to his legs, he sensed a blur to his right as a foot long piece of lead pipe bounced off the back of his head and he was falling down the longest cliff in the world, one with a river at the bottom that he thought he never would hit.

Jim woke up swearing at the blasting ache in his head and the cramps in his arms and legs. For a moment he thought it must be night, then he realized he was under some kind of a blanket or a tarp. He pushed upward but it wouldn't budge. The swaying, jolting motion of a freight wagon broke through his harried brain and registered. He had been shanghaied! — clubbed from behind and run out of town on a wagon. Quickly he tried his hands again and discovered they were tied together in front of him. His feet were free.

Jim wiggled around as much as he could until he got his hands up to his mouth. It was a tough, quarter-inch rope that laced his hands together. He would never chew it apart. He tried to find the knots with his chin, then began to pull at the loops with his teeth. But was he tightening the knots or untying them? He needed light.

Toward his feet he saw a faint greyness that had to be the outside world. It couldn't be dark yet, so he had to get his head where his feet were. It was downhill and that helped. Now Jim realized the freight was tied securely under a canvas which he was lying on. The tarp over him was a second one, put on for his benefit, to cover him up until he was out of town. So the driver probably knew he was there. That meant yelling at him would do no good. He had to get untied and surprise the driver, get the rig turned around and back to town.

It took him a half hour to squirm around so he could find enough light to work on the knots. When he saw them he guessed that Ed himself must have done the rope work. The knots were simple and poorly done. He was glad a cow hand had not used the rope.

Five minutes after he had his head in the halt light he got the ropes off his wrists. It took another half hour to figure a way out of the canvas. At last he pulled his whittling knife out of his pocket and slowly sliced a hole in the tarp. Jim looked out cautiously. He had been tied near the back of the load, so he could get out and move up partway on the twenty-foot load of the heavy freight wagon before the driver could see him. When Jim poked his head up over a large hump of freight, a hot-lead slug sang so close over his head he could smell the gunpowder.

"Howdy, there, pardner. Boss told me you'd be waking up."

Jim looked at the red-shirted teamster. He didn't know the man, and he was sure the money he had with him had gone long before this time. Jim still held the knife. He slowly closed the blade and put it in his pocket.

"Mind if I ride up there with you?" Jim asked.

"I don't mind, but the boss told me to keep you back there."

"You work for Percival?"

"Danged if I don't. Thought most everyone in Bisbee did."

"I don't."

The teamster laughed, but the gun kept trained on Jim's third shirt button. "No, I reckon you don't. He told me to let you off anywhere around here. You had a dandy sleep, now it's a fifteen mile walk back to town. You want that I should stop?"

Jim considered it. Fifteen miles. The sun would be down soon. He could walk it before morning, and there was one water hole half way there.

"Yeah, stop them."

When the four horses had pulled up, Jim stepped down muscle weary and cramped. He looked up at the driver.

"Got a canteen?"

"Yep, got my own."

"How about one for me?"

"It's only fifteen miles. A saddle jockey like you shouldn't need no water in that short piece."

Before Jim could argue the big man had whipped the blacks into motion down the trail toward Lordsburg. Jim threw a stone after the vanishing wagon. They had even thought to send him back East fifteen miles, to put him that much farther from the action.

Jim began walking. As he walked he thought, and a hundred times, that first mile, he thought how childish he had been to go to see Ed Percival at all. He might have guessed the outcome of any refusal — if he had thought it through far enough.

The country was bleak, dry, little more than desert with an occasional hill, arroyo and stunted sage. The stage trail was plain enough, and when the sun dropped behind the western hills it was even pleasant for a few minutes. He picked out a hill mass ahead of him for a guidepoint as dusk fell and used it to walk toward. There was no moon but he could follow the tracks in the sand.

As he walked he calculated the time. He had been put off the wagon about six in the evening, and as the first stars winked out he guessed the time at almost nine. He had been walking three hours and at even two miles an hour. . . . He sat down on a slab of rock beside the trail. Had he missed the double wash the stage trail cut across and the water hole just beyond it? He tried to look around but it was too dark. The teamster could have been off on his estimate — they could have been closer to twenty miles from town.

Jim walked again. Now he was swearing at the riding boots he wore. A lot of good those small heels did him now. He wasn't bulldogging a cow or riding down a rope digging his heels in to slow down the critter. Next time he got to town he was going to buy a pair of flat-heeled walking boots. He didn't care how funny they looked.

An hour later he found the water hole. It was a small spring that seeped from behind a pair of boulders at the edge of a wash. In dry weather the spring made a foot deep sink, then the overflow was lost in the thirsty sand of the wash. No one had fixed the spring to make a permanent watering place. Any work done one day could be wiped out the next by a thunderstorm, or a cloudburst which swept down from angry skies. Then the spring would start to build up a new wet sink and after a few days a small pool was formed.

He drank, washed the dust from his face and arms, and drank again. He thought of sleeping there, waiting for the morning stage which would be going past there about five a.m. But his stubborn pride wouldn't let him be seen walking in the desert, begging for a ride. He'd walk in under his own power, and he'd see Ed Percival in jail an hour after he was in town.

With the thought of putting Percival behind bars, he swung away from the spring, refreshed and ready for the rest of his stroll to town. The spring was eight miles from town, which should be four hours. He didn't want to think how big the blisters would be.

It was just after two a.m. by the stars when Jim took the last step up to the boardwalk and pushed open the door of the sheriff's office. He hadn't locked it when he left and it didn't look like anyone had been there since he left with such high-minded intentions. He closed the door, locking it now and finding the bunk where he had slept so many nights. He slid off his boots, massaging his feet, then lay down and slept as soon as he closed his eyes. Come daylight he would rout Ed out of his den and throw him in jail so fast his fancy women would think a thunderstorm had hit.

But he didn't waken at daylight. It was nearly eight o'clock before he turned over and noticed the sun coming through the window. Jim sat up slowly, moved his feet to the floor and swore. A huge blister had formed on the ball of each foot. He pricked them open with his knife, draining out the fluid, then soaked them in cold water until he thought he could walk on them.

The day before he had brought his gear from the hotel and put it in the jail, and now found he had used his last pair of clean socks. He slid his used ones on and then carefully worked his sore feet into the leather boxes.

Jim was hungry enough to chew on slabs of raw horsemeat by the time he got to the cafe and worked over the ham and eggs they were serving. Every chair was filled when he left the eatery.

Jim went into the office by the back door and sat near the window looking at the Star and Garter. How did he get Percival? He couldn't just barge in the front door, or the fat little man would scurry out the back door and hide.

That was when he remembered the bank. Percival went to the bank every morning just after it opened at ten. He took in the night's receipts. Ed was a creature of habit, and Jim was sure this would be no different than every other morning. All he had to do was wait until the little man waddled out of the bank with the heavy satchel and the two armed guards. The two men wouldn't do anything on Main street, especially when a deputy sheriff was making a legal arrest.

Jim wrote out the complaint and had it all ready to file with the county clerk as soon as he picked up his prisoner.

By ten fifteen Percival hadn't left his saloon. Jim had started to worry when the little man pushed open the doors and came out. Both he and one of the guards carried satchels this time.

Jim let them get half way to the bank, in front of the hardware store before he left the office and with his gun drawn, shouted across the street. "Percival, hold it right there, you're under arrest!"

The small man turned, talking quietly to his guards. He turned toward Jim.

"Now, Deputy, surely you're not going to let a little practical joke. . . ."

Before he finished the sentence one of the guards had turned and fired at Jim. His aim was wild and before he could get off another shot Jim's Colt roared and the slug caught the assassin as he was squeezing the trigger. He fell backwards and his gun spit two bullets at the sky before he died. The other guard had reached for his gun, but now held his hands in plain sight of the sheriff.

Jim ran toward them, his smoking gun never wavering from the fat man. Jim took the gun from the second guard and pushed him back against the building. He took a derringer from an inside pocket of Percival. A curious crowd had gathered now. Jim raised his voice so they all could hear.

"Ed Percival, I'm arresting you on a warrant charging you with assault and battery, with kidnapping and attempted murder."

"What? A practical joke, Sheriff, that's all it was. And how'd you get a warrant so fast, judge isn't even in town?"

"You can worry about it from your jail cell, now move."

Jim took the two bags of money and locked them in the jail safe, and put Percival in the worst cell of the six. When the lock was turned, Jim hung the big key on the hook.

"Now, fat little man, you stew in your own juices for a while. I may be back this afternoon to see if you're cooked." Jim went out, closing the window shutter and locking it, then closing the main door and locking it.

He couldn't even hear Percival's shouts any more.

As Jim walked down the street toward Luke's house he saw Kathy digging at some flowers in the front yard, looking toward him. She had been waiting for him.

He lifted her by the elbow when he came beside her and they went inside without a word.

"How's Luke?" he asked after she closed the door behind them.

"Better. Healing some, getting mean."

"That's a good sign."

She seemed nervous. "Jim, about the other night. . . ."

He laughed and kissed her forehead. "Don't worry about it, you're my girl, aren't you?"

"Am I?"

"You sure are. Now let's see the old man."

Luke was watching the door.

"Heard you come in, wondered how long you two would take before you came in to see the patient."

"She tells me you're getting mean."

"Not mean enough." He looked up at Jim's badge but didn't say anything about it. Jim saw a look of relief sweep over him.

"Oh, got a letter wanted to tell you about. From Pinkerton."

"Pinkerton? What those Jaspers want?"

"Me."

"What?"

"Yep, want me to go to work for them in Houston."

"Texas?"

"Was, last time I knew."

"Why?"

"Oh, just figured I'd had enough of this sheriff rigamarole. . . ."

"And you can't shoot, right? Hell, you don't have to be able to shoot to be sheriff. Hire yourself a couple of men with guns and you sit on your tail in the office. Look at the Eastern sheriffs — they don't even know what a gun is."

"Offered me good money."

"You wouldn't like it. Inside work, monotonous."

Luke's eyes sparkled. "Well, never knew you liked the sheriff business so much. Maybe you should just stay on here with that badge."

Jim laughed and sat down in the chair beside the bed. "Okay you trapped me."

He frowned at Luke, then looked at Kathy. "He really get an offer from Pinkerton?"

"Yes, but it was from Philadelphia."

"Ha, you old lying coot! You wouldn't even know which spoon to use."

"Which one?"

"Sure, they put down three spoons beside your plate in them fancy hotels where them Pinkerton detectives stay. And you don't use the right spoon. . . . Wham! They pitch you right out into the street."

"Do tell?"

"I'm getting this town in shape for you. Time you get out of bed next week you can take over. I'll have Ed Percival half way to the territorial prison at Yuma and I'll have Red Paulson dug under at boothill."

The name sobered the conversation.

"Seen him?"

"I see him and he'll be dead."

"Or you will be, Jim," Kathy said.

"Girl, don't talk that way. This is man's work."

She ran from the room, hands over her face.

"She'll get over it," Luke said gruffly. "Look, don't take no chances with Red. Don't matter none now."

"You worry about the getting well, leave the law work to me." Jim moved toward the door. "Don't go running off anywhere now," he said and went into the living room.

Kathy left the couch and ran to him, her arms holding him tightly.

"I'm sorry," she said through her tears.

"All my life I've heard about guns and killing and vengeance. And every time that man's name is mentioned Dad gets so hateful I can hardly stand it."

"Don't worry about it, Kathy," he said softly, kissing the tears away from her eyes. "That's man's work, you just stay soft and pretty and keep that smile on your face.

Jim watched her pretty face try to smile. It couldn't quite do the job, as if she knew she should be crying instead.

CHAPTER TEN

When Jim got back to the jail just before noon, he heard Ed Percival yelling even before the door lock clicked open. Jim hustled a couple of loafers down the boardwalk, then went in and yelled at Percival to quiet down if he wanted anything to eat.

"You get fed twice a day if you behave yourself," Jim growled at Percival. "And I just might put some ground up glass in what you do get."

Jim ate at the cafe that noon, and brought back a plate of stew and two slabs of bread for Percival.

"Eat it or starve," Jim said, pushing it in the door. "I don't care which you do."

That afternoon Jim closed up the jail again, double locked the doors and windows and sat at the desk with a loaded double-barreled Greener across his lap. He really didn't expect any trouble with Ed's boys, but he was ready.

There was no word from the army wagon. Tomorrow, Jim decided. When nothing happened with Percival before nine that evening, Jim collapsed into his bunk.

Morning dawned bright and cheerful, with a pile of thunderheads on the horizon but not much chance of any showers. Jim fed Percival and told him to sweat it out until about four when he'd be back from a short ride.

Before Jim had the front door locked the best lawyer in town, J. Andy Browning, stopped him.

"Oh, Deputy, I've got a release order here for my client who I believe you have incarcerated."

Jim remembered him from before — a snooty dude. The paper was right, a bail order, signed by the municipal judge and paid and signed by the city clerk.

"He's all yours, but don't stand close, he don't smell none too good this morning."

Ed Percival glowed with white hot anger as he stalked out of the cell. He turned to Jim but couldn't get the words out. Still sputtering and stammering, Ed Percival marched across the street, and into the Star and Garter without a glance to either side. Jim had an idea he was trying to be invisible until he had taken a bath, put on clean clothes, and had a big helping of wine and women.

Jim locked the jail door and brought his buckskin around saddled and ready to ride. Jim got only as far as the west edge of town when he saw the dust trail. For a moment it looked like a Texas trail herd going north. The dust rose high into the blue sky, obscuring some of the thunderheads that seemed to be stationary ten miles on the west.

The column was a mile out of town, so Jim waited for it. As the lead scouts turned south of town he counted. At least forty-eight troopers on horses and three four-harness army freight wagons, riding low to the ground. After they had passed Jim rode toward the area and checked the tracks. The wheels had dug in deep in the softer dirt when they cut cross-country to go south of town. They were loaded with something.

The phrase from Dan Barton's letter came back to him as he looked at the tracks. "Think small and don't plan for a large celebration." Jim kicked Hamlet and moved the buckskin west. Now he knew what his trooper buddy Barton had meant about thinking small. All of the gold was on one wagon!

That had to be the answer. A small celebration must mean that, along with the fact of very few armed men along, maybe no mounted escort at all! Sure why not? Two or three men on a wagon, heavily loaded but sticking to the known roads and rolling along a few miles a day, slow, steady, attracting no attention, letting the Red Paulsons worry about the big armed escort jobs like the one that just went through town.

Jim rode out toward the west now with more confidence than he had felt in days. He thought he knew something the others didn't. Only time would tell. He followed the main wagon track that went to Tucson.

First he met a farm wagon, some farmer-rancher trying to scratch out a living in one of the small valleys. The second rig was a freight wagon out of Tucson, but it was almost empty — going into Bisbee to pick up a load of goods.

He rode five miles, looking as far down trail as he could. Nothing. On the way back to town he tried to decide how he would disguise a wagon hauling a ton of gold. First he would strip it of every non-essential to cut the weight so it would ride somewhat normally. Then put on his trappings.

He leaned toward a real fire and brimstone evangelist. A traveling preacher who ranted and raved about being saved by the Blood of the Lamb. That usually ran the people away. He would put the gold under a false bottom in the wagon bed and roll right past the gold snatchers and the regular army lookouts and everyone! Great, but first he had to find the gold.

He saw no more wagons on his way back into town, but he did look over critically every rig he saw on four wheels. Jim swung into the hitching rail outside the sheriff's office and dropped off his mount. He checked the tack board near the office door and saw no urgent messages for him. He mounted again and rode the block and a half to Luke's house. If Jim noticed anything unusual about the place it didn't register consciously. He knocked on the door and waited a minute.

Nothing happened. He knocked again and thought he heard some movement inside. His gun was in his hand quickly and he turned the door knob and pushed it open, stepping to one side. No shots came through the open door, no sound. Jim looked cautiously around the door jamb and saw Luke lying on the kitchen floor.

He rushed into the kitchen, lifting Luke's head off the floor. The sheriff's eyes were open. He waved his good arm limply toward the door.

"Kathy. Somebody took Kathy!"

He looked out the door, but saw no riders, no buggy.

"How long ago, Luke? When?"

"I don't know. Two hours, maybe. Tried to stop them. They didn't like that. Hit me."

Now Jim saw the ugly scrape where a six gun had slammed across Luke's forehead, gouging out skin and flesh.

"Who was it, Luke?"

"Masked. Don't know. Didn't know the voices. Told Kathy to go with them or they'd finish me. She went."

"How many men, Luke?"

"Three. Two in here, one at the door." He struggled to sit up. Sweat streamed off his face from the effort. "Jim, they left a message for you. Said you had to do three things if you ever wanted to see Kathy alive. Said to get out of town within an hour. To forget why you came to Bisbee and to never come back."

He slumped forward with the effort. Jim picked him up and carried him back to his bed. As they moved Jim questioned him again. The sick man hadn't seen what direction they went when they left.

As soon as Jim had Luke comfortable again, he ran to the house next door. Mrs.

144

MacFarland promised to go stay with Luke until someone got back. She said she did see four riders heading down the street toward the school two hours ago.

Jim thanked her and rode toward the school. He knocked on every door, and asked about the four horsemen. Two women were sure the riders had gone due southwest out of town. One wondered what Kathy was doing riding with three men. No, she had never seen the men before. She watched them out of sight and was sure they were going toward the old ice pond and quarry down on Quarry road. Jim thanked them and rode down the street until it turned into Quarry road. Now he could see the four sets of prints plainly. He swung low in the saddle looking at the ground, but there were no distinguishing points about the tracks, only four fresh made ones heading southwest.

He turned his buckskin back to town. At the sheriff's office he picked up his bedroll and tied it and his small war bag behind it on his saddle. He scribbled a note for the door that said "I quit as Deputy. Moving East." He signed it and hammered two tacks into it on the door.

He rode out of town to the east without a word to anyone. Soon as he was beyond the range of any field glasses, he picked a large wash that led south and rode into it. He stayed in the bottom of the wash, crossed to another ravine and worked around until he was due south of Bisbee, then he came up to flat ground and rode hard for the Quarry road. He was a mile beyond where he had left the four sets of tracks, but he found them quickly on the road.

They were making it too easy. He let Hamlet have a blow as he sat side-saddle and built a smoke, took a half a dozen drags on it and snubbed it out on the saddle. It was a trap. He had to circle and come up behind the quarry. But he was still four miles from the big hole in the side of the hill where they had blasted out rock to build the courthouse. He had gone to the trouble of the ritual of leaving town so someone could see him. Maybe he should stay out of sight for an hour or so and see what happened? It was the best plan. He moved along until he found another good sized wash crossing the trail, and rode up it two hundred yards where it bent enough so he could hide the buckskin.

He tied Hamlet to a scrub bush and crawled up to the lip of the wash and watched his back trail. Lying there in the warm afternoon sun he dozed once, roused and looked back at the trail again. This time he saw a thin plume of dust rising and moving his way. A half hour later the rider went past on the quarry road at an easy trot. Jim couldn't identify the man, but he wore a big red neckerchief around his throat. He watched the rider move down the trail almost to the outcropping, then turn left and work his way to the top of the hill that fronted the quarry.

Jim had been all over that hill and this area. There was no place there to camp. They must be behind the quarry some place, or maybe they had a lookout in front of it who would talk to the messenger. Jim figured the rider must be from town, telling them Jim had ridden out, cleared out of town.

Jim pulled his hat down over his eyes and rested his head on his arms. He had nothing to do but wait, now, wait until the messenger came back, or until it got dark. What he should be doing was sitting on a hill someplace west of here watching for that gold wagon on the Tucson trail. He kicked the toe of one boot into the ground in frustration. He was locked in now, and there wasn't a damn thing he could do about it.

He had been sleeping and waking and sleeping again for two hours before the sun settled behind the hills in front of him. Another half hour and he could ride without attracting any attention. In an hour it would be dark. He wanted to be close to the hill by then. Jim guessed they would pull their lookout off the hill, once they found out Jim had blown out of town. They would hold Kathy and celebrate a little tonight, then take her back to town tomorrow.

At least they wouldn't be on guard tonight. That would make his job easier.

It took him an hour to ride cautiously to the hill, then another half hour to work up the slope to the spot he figured the lookout had used. There was no one there, only a sack that had contained food, and some cigarette butts. Jim walked back ten yards to the lip of the cliff that had been blasted away. He could look across the black hole of the quarry, and to the slope on the far side that climbed to the top of the hill a mile away. He didn't remember any water holes in this section. There might be a sink that would hold run-off water. In the winter the quarry filled with enough water for them to saw out ice for the ice houses. But not now.

Jim lay on the rim looking into the surrounding area, watching for any flicker of light, listening for any noise.

He saw the fire almost at once. It was on the far left. As he remembered the area had a few stunted pines and some brush. Jim worked his way down the mountain soundlessly, circled to the left and came up behind where he estimated the camp site would be. He missed it by ten yards. As Jim moved he felt like he was back in the army, crawling up on an enemy outpost, with a long knife between his teeth for a silent attack.

This was different. He could hear the plaintive song one of the men sang as he plucked at an out-of-tune guitar. When he edged under a branch he could see the camp. It was not new, and must have been used for months by someone. The guitar picker had his back to Jim as he leaned against a tree. A second man seemed sleeping on a blanket near the fire. The third man was cleaning his gun by the light of the fire, and a fourth talked in low tones with Kathy. He could see that her ankles were tied together, but her hands were free.

"Hey, Cholla, told you you'd never get her blouse off, not and keep your eyes," the man with the guitar said.

The kidnapper near Kathy didn't let on he heard, just went on talking to the girl softly. His hand rested on her shoulder then moved down. Kathy screamed and clawed his face, and the man jumped back in surprise.

His movement gave Jim a safe shot. His six gun had been out and now only the faint click of the hammer cocking sounded before Jim shot the man in the chest and saw him thrown to his back. Even before the sound of the shot had died away Jim was shouting.

"Hold it all of you, right there. I've got six men around you and anybody moves is a dead man." Those in the fire light froze, realizing their mistake. "You three men, stand slowly, drop your guns where you stand. We'd just as soon shoot you all right here and save the county the cost of a trial." Jim had picked up a fist-sized rock. Now he threw it to one side to simulate some movement. The rock snapped a branch and Jim was on top of it.

"Hold it men, give them a chance!" Jim said sharply. One of the men had hesitated about giving up his gun, but after the exchange he lay it in the dust and stood.

"Over against the rocks," Jim ordered. When they were at the edge of the light Jim stopped them. "Guitar picker, go slowly to the girl and cut the rope on her ankles. You even nick her skin and you're buzzard food."

The man did as he was told, then went

back with the others and faced the rocks.

"Lady, can you walk?" Jim asked.

He saw Kathy nod. "Then get up and walk toward my voice. Men, keep the others covered." Jim watched the three carefully, this was the critical point. As she moved one of them might. His glance was on Kathy as she stood but the movement to his left made him swing his gun that direction. The man who had been sleeping had pulled a derringer from his shirt and was aiming for Kathy.

Jim's first shot caught him in the thigh and spun him around. The second slug from Jim's Colt bored through his chest and he slammed backwards against the rock, then he slid downward slowly, not moving.

"Hold your fire!" Jim yelled. Kathy, who had been moving, slumped to the ground at the shots, now she stood and ran toward him in the darkness.

Jim ordered one of the men in the firelight to tie up the other one, then he tied the first and checked the knots. Both of them would be safe until morning.

In the darkness again he found Kathy sobbing softly. She put her arms around him and clung tightly.

"It's all right now, *muchacha,* it's all over." He kissed her cheek, then her lips and it

151

seemed to shake off her fear.

"Where did they put the horses?"

Five minutes later they both had mounted and were riding toward where Jim had left his buckskin. Kathy came alongside him and smiled in the soft darkness.

"That's another time you've rescued the Tabor family," she said.

He laughed softly as he changed horses, then whacked the unneeded nag and watched it gallop away. "One of these days, lady, I'm going to settle accounts with you."

CHAPTER ELEVEN

They rode for three hours heading northwest, crossed the Tucson trail about midnight and angled north of it to a cluster of cedar trees growing on a small bench below a towering mountain. For many years it had been known as Cedar Springs, and was thought to be one of the earliest Indian water holes in this part of the southwest. But when the new stage road went through to include a small community, it cut off the springs from regular use. Now only an occasional traveler used the sweet water and the shade of the cedars.

Jim made a quick camp, showing Kathy how to roll up in the two blankets to shut out the chill of the desert night. He built a small fire, shielded from sight below by two big slabs of rock some long forgotten man had shoved into position, a one-hour fire, watching the sticks burn and turn to embers, then slowly flake away into white ash.

Kathy had kissed him goodnight and dropped off to sleep almost before the fire was started. He had brought her here on purpose, deciding not to go right back into town to see what else Percival would try. He knew he couldn't stall too long. Luke would be frantic, and when Red Paulson found out for sure there was no gold on the army wagons, he would be back with his anger at an even more explosive level.

The gold wagon lay ahead, still on the trail somewhere toward Bisbee, he was sure of it. He looked at Kathy and remembered all of the time he had lost taking care of her and Luke these past few days. But as he watched the way she slept in the soft glow of the fire his regret faded, and he knew he wanted to learn more about this girl-child who had grown up in three years into a provocative and interesting woman.

The embers of the fire burned lower and lower. He checked the stars and saw that it must be almost two in the morning. Jim bunched his coat around his shoulders and lay back against a slab of rock that still held the warmth of the day's sun.

When he awakened, Jim smelled coffee. Before he opened his eyes he could hear her moving around on quiet feet, softly humming to herself.

"Good morning," he said.

"Hi, coffee is almost ready," she said looking down at him. "You snore."

He laughed and stood, dusting himself off down-wind, then adding some small, dry sticks to the fire to hold down the smoke and wishing he'd taken time to get some bacon before he'd left. They settled for beans and coffee and half a hard biscuit they found in the saddlebag. Kathy topped it with a drink of the clean, pure water.

"This is a beautiful spot," she said.

"Get used to it, we'll be staying here a while."

She glanced up mischievously. "From one kidnapper to another one?"

He reached for her and pulled her down on his lap. "Right, and I'm going to assault you and tease you and do all sorts of wild, wicked things to your body."

Before he could say another word, her lips had closed over his and her kiss was hot. He pulled back. "Yes, I just might do all of those things, but first I've got some work to do."

He pushed her off his lap and scooped up sand with his hands to put out the fire. Next he took her fifty feet up the slope, to the highest point still concealed by the cedars.

"That's what we're watching, the road to Tucson," he said.

"For that gold wagon that's never coming?"

"Oh, it's coming."

"And you're going to turn outlaw and steal the gold?"

"I figure the army still owes me some back pay. If they make a mistake and overpay me, I won't tell them about it."

"That's just as dishonest."

"Kathy I tried being honest, and I was thrown in jail three times for murder. I'm through with that."

"But robbery?"

"Forget all about it. All you have to do today is stay cool and drink all the Cedar Springs dry if you can." He had brought a blanket. He spread it out and stood up. "I want to make a quick check around the area. Shouldn't be gone more than an hour. If anybody comes, lay low and don't let them see you. If they come this way, hide." He grinned. "Does that scare you?"

"A little."

"That's the way to stay alive, stay a little scared." He turned and jogged down the trail. A moment later she heard him ride out. She saw him several times during the next hour, as he nosed in and out of depressions below. Then he was gone, and she breathed a sigh of relief when she saw the big buckskin bringing him back up the hill. But she stayed at the lookout point. So far she had seen only three things that were moving. One buzzard, soaring high in the blue sky to the north; a small lizard that crawled close to her, his black eyes darting, and his body springing up, then squatting in some type of strange dance. He was only three inches long, and silently she hoped that he were fully grown.

The other sign of life was a single horseman, walking his mount towards Bisbee. He was about half way across her area of vision now, making steady progress. He made no move to come up to the springs.

"An Indian," Jim said from directly behind her.

"Oh," she said surprised. "I didn't hear you come up."

"Wonder where he's going."

"How can you tell it's an Indian?"

"No saddle, long hair," he said.

"You find anything?"

He shook his head. "Not a trace, they still must be down the trail."

They stayed until noon. But nothing else materialized from the desert haze that settled down, making the mountains dance in shimmering waves of heat.

They ate the last two cans of beans for lunch and packed the blankets.

"Time to go home," Jim said. "We can wait a lot easier at your place."

They rode. It took them four hours to get back to town, and Kathy was hot, tired, dirty and wanting a bath.

Jim saw her to the door, briefed Luke on what happened at the old quarry and went to his office. He wrote out a complaint on kidnapping, naming two John Does, and tacked it on the board. Then he went looking for Abe Daltan, one of the men who had gone out with the posse the first morning he was here. Abe was the hardware store owner, and he was just closing up. Jim explained what he needed, and Abe said he and his eighteen-year-old son could do the job. One of them would be on guard inside the sheriff's house all the time.

When Jim got back to the office a pimply-face boy was waiting for him. He handed Jim a note and scurried into the alley. He went inside, lit the lamp and read the note.

"Meet me at the cafe, right now."

It wasn't signed but he recognized the handwriting. It was from Adele. Jim turned the note over twice in his hands before he read it again. He suspected everything as

158

being a trap. They could have forced her to write the note. He inspected his six-gun and slid it back into leather. Either way he had to go check it out.

The cafe was jammed when he got there. He took a plate of steak and potatoes and found an empty place at the counter. He had taken only one bite from the steak when he found Adele at his side.

"Back here," she said, picking up his plate and fork and leading him behind the counter into the storeroom of the small eatery.

He sat down at a box and went on eating the steak and potatoes and carrots.

"We've found that item you've been hunting," Adele said.

"Where?"

"Can't say, you with us?"

Jim bit into another mouthful of steak and let her wait. When he had swallowed he shook his head. "It ain't coming from the west, that's where I been."

"North. My boys spotted it, been following it for two days. They say it's got to be the one."

"Why?"

"One, no big escort, two riders, no uniforms. The wagon is set up like a tinsmith's rig, loaded with sheet metal, benders, pots and pans, the works. It looks phony as hell."

"Lots of things look phony, why do you think it has the right cargo?"

"First day we watched it a blue-shirted trooper appeared out of nowhere, gave the driver an envelope and took off so fast they hardly knew he was there. So far they've been skirting all little camps and towns, but sticking close to the road."

Jim took another bite of steak.

"Well, what do you think?"

"Sounds possible, but don't shoot the three and ask questions later."

"You don't want to come along?" she asked.

"Why?"

"For that 10 percent."

"Don't make sense they'd come in from the north. Why not move on toward Lordsburg, lots quicker?"

"Let's go ask them."

Jim took another bite of the steak, then peeled off the prime eating from the middle and stood up. "I'll go, just so you let me finish this on the way."

It took Jim a half hour to get his saddle bags repacked and his blankets shaken out, and it was full dark when he and Adele jogged out of town on the north road. They rode for an hour before coming to a small fire near the road, and the five hands. Jim found Duke Jannis, the man he'd knocked down at the Star and Garter.

"Duke, no hard feelings about that sneak punch I hit you with the other day?"

Duke frowned at him from deep brown eyes. Then shrugged. "I got over it."

"Good, Duke." He lowered his voice. "Duke, you look like the only man here who I could rely on in case of trouble. You stick with me."

Duke nodded and they killed the fire and rode north. They found the wagon just off the road on a rocky spot. The three men had built a large campfire, a smaller one for cooking and had settled down.

Jim had ordered his men off horses a half mile away and worked his motley crew to the site on foot. Jim circled and looked at the wheels and wheelprints, they didn't seem heavy enough for the load he could see hanging on the covered wagon type rig.

Jim told the others to stay where they were and not to shoot. He edged closer until he could pick up the conversation. The more he listened the more convinced he was they were not soldiers disguised as tinsmiths. The men used none of the military flavored language, and they didn't talk about the current project.

A half hour later Jim had returned to the group which had found positions commanding the semi-circle where the rig could get back on the road. He sent the youngest of the crew running back for his horse and told the boy to ride him slowly to the rock just behind them.

"I'm going to ride in and chew the fat with them for a while," Jim said. "They look as harmless as a pair of turtle doves on a rainspout."

Adele shook her head. "Nope, that's the wagon, got to be. Everything matches. No escort, slip through towns, attract no attention. Got to be them."

When his horse came Jim galloped him into the camp, walking the last fifty feet, careful to make lots of noise. He didn't see a single weapon as he rode up.

"Hello there, travelers. This the road to Lordsburg?"

The oldest of the men stood and shook his head. "Afraid not, stranger. You missed a turn five, ten miles back there, maybe more. This one goes to Bisbee."

"Dang, guess I'll have to go back."

"Had your supper yet?"

"Well, now, that's mighty kind of you. Could stand a few mouthfuls."

"Got some good possum soup all ready, I'll heat it up a mite."

Jim relaxed, watching the men. They were southern, for sure. "You guys real tin-smiths?"

"Real as they come," the third man said. "Figuring on opening up a store in Bisbee. Know the place?"

Jim flipped back his jacket showing his badge. "Fact is I do, gents. I'm the deputy sheriff there. Looking for a pair of sneak thieves who stole over a thousand dollars worth of jewels from the hotel."

He waited but the men didn't show any unfamiliar reactions. One laughed. Another one frowned and spat on the ground.

"If you don't mind, I'd like to look over your wagon. Now, isn't my idea. The sheriff told me to check out every wagon and rider I found around here."

The older man nodded. "Course, Sheriff. Just do your duty. We're law abiding men." He followed Jim to the wagon. "Oh, is there a tinsmith in Bisbee? We're hunting a place to settle down."

Jim told him about the old man who had worked there but died two years back. Jim found nothing in the wagon but what he expected, and the wheels rode the softer ground easily. He got out and nodded to

163

the three.

"Sorry to trouble you. You see anybody looking sneaky you remember him for me."

Jim swung into the saddle and waved. "Probably see you in Bisbee." He rode out and into the darkness, heading down trail toward Bisbee. He rode slowly and in a few minutes the rest of the group caught him.

"Well, what did you find?" Adele demanded.

Jim turned toward her with a touch of anger in his eyes. He wanted to lash out at her, to accuse her of being a decoy for Ed Percival. He wasn't sure of that, but it certainly loomed as a strong possibility.

"I found nothing, they're three tinsmiths going to Bisbee to open up a business. Let's get the hell back to town!"

CHAPTER TWELVE

Jim led the long, silent ride back to town. The men behind were talking, grumbling, one small argument broke out but Jim didn't catch what it was about.

Jim pulled them up just outside of town.

"You men have anything to say to the lady who's been paying your wages?" he asked.

Most of them stared at the ground, or adjusted the reins in their hands. At last Duke Jannis looked up.

"I'm through, Miss Adele. I've had enough sitting around waiting. Time I headed out and looked for an honest job."

Four of the others nodded, saying they'd had enough, too.

Adele shrugged. "Maybe it was a crazy idea, anyway."

Adele kicked the flanks of her mare and rode out alone into town.

Jim watched her go, waiting until Jannis rode up.

"Duke? See you a minute?" Jim asked.

They rode together down the street and Jim put it to him straight.

"I want you to be a deputy. Ever been a lawman before?"

"No."

"Let's go talk to the sheriff. I think you can do the job, and I don't think you'd let Red Paulson scare you off."

Duke rode straight ahead, evidently thinking about it. He turned toward Jim. "Backing you?"

"For a while, and being the gun hand for Sheriff Luke Tabor. He can't even fist a gun anymore."

Duke nodded. "Yeah. I could settle down, maybe help clean up this town."

"Come on, let's go see the sheriff."

It was two hours later that Jim had his chores finished. He put his buckskin in the livery and gave him a good feed of oats, then bunked down in the office. Duke Jannis had been sworn in by Luke and now took a turn at walking the night streets of Bisbee. Jim hoped he had an easy night. He had told Duke everything he would need to know, and a lot extra. Now it was up to the young man to prove himself. Jim had no doubt he would, as he turned over and went to sleep.

■ ■ ■ ■

By ten the next morning Jim had his buckskin outfitted for the road. He filled the
saddlebags for a week's trip, said goodbye
to Duke, then rode out of town quickly
before he changed his mind and went back
to see Luke and Kathy. If he came back, it
would be time enough to worry about
Kathy. If he didn't, there would be no problem.

He rode hard, moving quickly out the
Tucson trail and up the edge of the hills
toward Cedar Springs. No one had touched
his small camp. He had met no one on the
road. Now it begins, Jim thought, the long
wait, the do-or-die time when his plans all
worked out or blew up in his face.

Jim scanned the road until it faded into
the haze around the far slopes and went to
the spring to wash and have a drink. The
thunderheads he had been riding toward
had broken up and drifted into thin stream-
ers high in the sky. He frowned, knowing
they needed rain. The cattle on the sparse
hillsides would welcome the surge of new
grass it would bring, and the whole area
could stand a washing down.

It had to come soon, with the buildup of

the thunderheads every day. But he hoped it rained slow enough so some could soak into the ground. The gully-washers turned the washes into sudden raging rivers that could send a wall of water three feet high smashing downstream.

Jim made a small fire from the bone-dry sticks and dead cactus, making sure that the wood made no more than the faintest trace of smoke. He cooked a slab of ham he had brought with him, and coffee. The ham went between inch-thick slabs of home-made bread he had brought. Then he ate.

All afternoon he watched the trail, sleeping in cat-naps, rousing and sweeping the long expanse of trail but finding it empty, then going back to sleep again.

The sun came down like the business end of a blowtorch. He had the cedars for shade and plenty of cold water, but he was sweating like a sway-back horse in a two-mile race every time he woke. His plan was to keep the road under guard from this point all day, then at dusk he would move down to the trail and watch and listen for anyone passing. He had no idea if the wagon would be moving during the day or night.

Jim took a look at the expanse of hot, dry land in front of him. A semi-desert, it held a few green spots, but mostly was sage and a flush of chaparral here and there in washes and ravines. The stage road curved around the bend in the hills to the left, swung a mile in front of his perch angling to the north sharply and vanishing in the haze toward the abandoned Fort Campstone. He guessed he could watch twelve miles of trail from his vantage point. Nobody was going to sneak a gold wagon past him.

That night he spent in a small wash behind a giant rock, listening for travelers. Two horsemen came through just after midnight, letting their horses walk, then jogging out at a cautious pace. It was a dark night and the moon was playing tag with some black clouds. Jim saw the men hunched over their saddles, showing the effects of many hours of riding.

Sometime late in the night he slept, but jolted awake when he dreamed he heard a wagon. His eyes stared intently through the darkness but he could see nothing. No sounds came but a wailing night bird, and the lonesome howl of a coyote.

But he didn't go to sleep the rest of the night, and no travelers disturbed him. Before daylight he was back in his Cedar Springs camp, cooking a big breakfast of four eggs he had cracked and stored in a small jar before he left the store, bacon and more slabs of the homemade bread. At least he would eat well for a day or two.

Before noon the stage went through, followed by a freight wagon. Just after noon he saw another wagon coming, this one from Tucson. It was not a freight wagon, nor a covered wagon. At first he thought it was a farm wagon of some sort, but as it came closer he saw it was a half covered wagon. The covered top could be hiding anything. One man rode on the high seat. Jim watched it come into sharp focus through the shimmering heat. It was big enough, heavy enough. Even when it was two miles directly below him, he knew it could be the one. He saddled slowly, hating to leave the shade, but when he swung up, he was ready to go, mentally ready.

He came up behind the wagon, riding in the dust, then at the last cutting across a wide curve in the stage road to avoid the dust and catch them faster. He was fifty yards off when the rifle shot slashed in front of him.

"Hold it, stranger," a booming voice commanded from the back of the wagon. The team had stopped, so he pulled the buckskin to a stop fifty yards away.

"Don't go for your gun, mister, got your heart in my sights and no man alive can move faster than a rifle bullet. Just drop your iron in the dust there and get down on this side of your nag."

Jim had no choice. He wasn't worried. Once they saw his badge it would be all apologies. He slid off the horse and put his six gun on the ground. Only then did someone jump down from the back of the wagon. For a moment he wasn't sure if it was man or woman. The bib overalls covered the woman completely, with only her long hair giving him a hint of her gender.

"Walk over here, slow like," she ordered.

Jim looked back at his gun, shrugged and did as she said.

"We don't like strange men riding up behind our wagon, Mister. Now what's your business?"

He was close enough to see her now. She was human, after all, he decided. Jim estimated she was about forty, with a fleshy face dominated by a large, crooked nose and cheeks with red splotches of color on them. She was not fat, exactly. But even at her five-feet-four-inch size she must have weighed 180 pounds. The rifle never wavered from Jim's chest as he walked toward her leading his horse.

"Morning, Ma'am. Didn't mean to scare you none."

"Don't matter, just keep your hands still. I ain't shot nobody in a week, but my trigger finger still knows how."

"Would you put down the rifle? My name is. . . ."

"Don't hold much with names. What you want?"

"I'm deputy sheriff from Bisbee, just heading back to town."

"I done heared that one before. You after what I got in my wagon?"

Jim tensed, then relaxed, this was ridiculous. This old bag of bones couldn't possibly be a man, especially one guarding a gold shipment. He laughed, slapping his hat on his leg. It was so funny he couldn't help himself. The rifle barked and dust flew up an inch to one side of his boot.

"I don't hold with men laughing at me, hear?" she screamed, her face going red with the effort.

Jim stopped laughing. Just another inch with that bullet. . . .

"Now, look. I don't know what you've got in your wagon, and I'm not interested. You took a shot at me first, remember? And about your wagon. I got a standing order from the sheriff in Bisbee to take a look in every wagon comes by here. We're watching for a pair of gunmen got themselves shot up some and can't ride. They maybe captured you and your wagon."

"Yeah? Then why you sneak up behind us?"

Before Jim could answer a girl parted the back flap of the wagon and stepped to the ground. She was blonde, wore a white blouse and tight riding trousers. When she turned her face was pretty — except for her nose which was a smaller version of her mother's.

"See, ma, told you he was nobody to be afraid of." She turned toward him. "You want to look inside this dumb old bake oven, you just help yourself."

Jim tipped his hat. "Thank you, Miss, that's kindly of you." Before he could take a step in her direction another shot stabbed through the desert heat and dust spurted beside him.

"Hold it!"

"Oh, Ma! First good lookin' man I seen in a month, and you keep shootin' at him."

"Shut up and get yourself back in that wagon."

As the two glared at each other, Jim saw another figure come around the back of the rig. Another girl. She wore men's pants, a workshirt, and a straw hat pulled down on her head that failed to cover up her dark black hair. She walked to the older woman, frowned at her for a moment, then gently took the rifle from her hands. She gave the weapon to the blonde and helped her mother toward the wagon. When the older woman was inside, she came back, the frown not quite gone from her round, plain face.

"I'm sorry ma got so riled, deputy. She's been a little touchy lately, ever since we got robbed and pa got killed about a month back."

Jim watched the girl as she talked and decided she wasn't plain, she was tired. She looked bone weary and ready to drop. He touched his hat brim again.

"Don't mention it, Miss. Anything I can do to help?"

The blonde girl in tight pants grinned. "Sure is! Why don't you ride back to Bisbee with us. That way you could spend a couple of nights with us. You know, protect us."

The dark eyes flashed anger at her blonde sister. "I'm sorry, Deputy, Martha is a real tease. She doesn't mean a word of it."

"Oh, yes I do, sister Amy. I mean every word of it. We need a man around here to protect us."

Jim wanted to laugh again, but he knew better this time. Martha seemed in the same

174

mold as her mother. He indicated his gun where he had put it down.

"I guess I'd better get my six-gun and not bother you folks no more." He turned, walking quickly to the spot where he left his iron. He found it and turned back toward the girls in time to see Martha push something under the saddle blanket and then pound down on the spot with her fist. The buckskin jumped, bellowed in pain and started running. Martha picked up the rifle and shot beside him as the pain-crazed critter took off across the sage, bucking, rearing, then running hard, trying to get rid of the hurting thing under the saddle blanket.

Jim was running now. He grabbed the rifle from Martha and threw it into the dirt.

"Now why'd you do that?" he demanded.

Martha smiled at him. "Guess?"

Amy stood, her hands on her hips glaring at Martha. "You may be my half-sister, but you're impossible!" She turned to Jim. "We can unhitch one of the team and you can ride after your horse."

"Do no such thing!" a voice cracked from the wagon. The older woman had stepped to the ground, this time she held a shotgun and Jim could see the hammer cocked. "Take his gun, Martha, then tie his hands behind him. We ain't gonna let this one go,

175

not like the last time. The Lord taken away, and now the Lord provideth. We ain't about to let this one get loose!"

"Ma, you cain't do that," Amy said. "He's a lawman. You keep him we can't go on into Bisbee."

"Don't matter, now we got a man. Don't matter where we go." The old woman laughed softly. "Yes sir, we sure have got us a man. You take a fancy to him, Martha?"

Martha had taken his gun and put it on the wagon, after she broke it open and took out the .44 rounds. Now she came back to Jim and walked around him slowly.

"Yeah, Ma, I think he'll do just fine. He's a mite tall and all, but I think he'll work out good."

"Ma, remember why we was going to Bisbee? We got kin there, your sister and her husband, remember? We got kin we can stay with, and help out, and they got two men in their family, you recall that, ma?"

For a moment the old woman's eyes hooded, then came wide.

"Yeah, but them men belong to them. This one is ours. We got him fair-square when he was a sneakin' up on our wagon!"

"He'll run away, Ma. Just like the other one."

The woman laughed, a long high cackle

that made Jim wince.

"Now, don't worry, chile, he won't do no such thing. Martha, go get 'em, them specials we got back down the trail a ways."

Martha laughed and jumped up the step and into the wagon. A moment later she threw down a pair of leg irons and a ten pound iron ball.

"He'll pay higher's hell's own to get away with these on," the old woman said, then laughed. "Ever see a man try to ride a horse with leg irons on? Downright amusing. Downright!"

The sun was half-way down in the afternoon sky before they got the leg irons in place. He had fought them, as best he could fight with two women. He pushed them away, kicked at the leg irons and the chains and kept out of their way for ten minutes. Then Martha had clouted him over the head with his own six gun handle and when the hive of bees stopped buzzing in his brain he found himself with leg irons and a ten pound ball padlocked to the chain.

Amy hadn't helped him during the first part, but now she was crying softly, and putting a damp cloth on his forehead. When she saw he was conscious, a fresh flood of tears came.

"Oh, thank the Lord, I was afraid they'd

killed you. I couldn't stop them. I wanted to, but I just couldn't."

He blinked his eyes back into focus and saw his hands tied in front of him. Using the back of his hand, he tried to rub the rest of the tangles away from his eyes.

"Those two always like this?"

She nodded, a spot of color showing in her cheeks. "That's why I want to get Ma to Bisbee and her sister. The whole family can help us tend her. It's too much for me, and Martha's not much help, especially when she. . . ." Amy paused. "She's at that man-crazy spell right now, I guess."

"Amy, I've got to get out of here, and you're the only one who can help me."

"But, I can't!"

"You can! There's nobody else. First, where's my horse? Find out how far he ran and talk them into letting you go get him. Tell them you want it for your own."

She nodded, and stood up from the shady side of the wagon.

"I'll try, but don't 'spect much."

The other two appeared then and helped him up the step and into the back of the wagon.

"Come on sweetie, time for a wagon ride," Martha said. She bent and kissed his cheek and laughed. "Now you just be a nice boy and we won't hurt you atall!" Then she left.

The inside of the wagon was poorly set up. Near the back, some blankets had been piled on the floor for a bed; boxes, sacks and one barrel sat near the front of the small wagon box.

As his mind cleared from the blow to his head, Jim tried to figure out the weird chain of events that put him in the hands of two women as a prisoner. He couldn't believe it had happened, from the first shot to the final blow from behind. He gritted his teeth now and looked at the chains. Somehow he had to get out of those damn things, and fast! For all he knew the gold wagon could have rumbled past two hours ago!

He felt the surge of new strength flow into his blood stream. His hands were first. At least they had tied them in front of him. They were tied with strips of cloth. He worked at the cloth furiously, tearing at it with his teeth. After five minutes of tugging and ripping he weakened enough of the bindings so he could unwind the last strands.

Now he looked around the inside of the wagon. Nothing here he could use on the irons. He was about to rise when he heard someone come around the wagon. He rolled over so his hands were under him, together with the cloth that had bound them.

He heard someone come in, then felt the hand on his leg and lips against his cheek. Something soft pressed against his shoulder.

"Not much longer to wait now. As soon as it gets dark I'll be back and we'll really do things!"

She pushed away then and went out of the wagon. It had been Martha. He shook his head. If she were that man-crazy he could get her a job in any saloon in Bisbee. They always needed an extra girl or two.

It was starting to get darker outside. Soon it would be dusk. He looked at the irons that locked around each ankle. He'd heard you could pick a lock like that with a piece of wire, but he'd never tried it. But where would he get wire? Then he looked again. These settler wagons usually carried a little of everything. On a nail in one of the roof bows he spotted a small coil of bailing wire. As quietly as he could he stood up and caught the coil, pulling it down. He bent one end and tried it in the lock, but nothing happened. He put another bend in the wire and tried it again.

It took him over thirty tries with various bends before he heard a light click and the lock opened. He thought the other iron would be the same, but the wire worked differently there. He tried it ten times without changing the pattern of the bends, then on an impulse twisted the wire the opposite way he had done on the first lock, and to his surprise the lock snicked open.

He could see a crack through the canvas opening outside. It was dusk now, in ten minutes it would be dark. Martha was singing somewhere in front of the wagon. He smelled smoke as a fire danced with freshly lit fury on the lee side of the white wagon top.

The shotgun? No it wasn't inside. He looked for a hand gun, or rifle, but found nothing. Cautiously he peeked through the rear opening only to have a face looking back at him.

It was Amy. He moved back, frowning with relief that it hadn't been the mother or Martha.

"I got your horse. He's tied to some sage. I couldn't find your gun. I think Ma's got it."

"Can you get rid of that rifle? Hide it or throw it away. Get rid of that and I'll make a run for the dark. Then I can get on that nag of mine and get away from here."

"I can't," she said starting to cry.

"Of course you can!" Jim said tensing

now, getting ready for his dash toward the home.

"No, I can't."

"Why not, Amy?"

Another face pushed into the wagon and with it came his own gun aimed at his stomach. Martha grinned at him.

"Because, man, if she does, I'll blow her brains out."

Jim grabbed the gun, holding tightly around the cylinders and at the same time jerking the surprised girl into the wagon. She yelped as he dragged her through the door, then his hand closed over her mouth. He was aware both of his arms were wrapped around her and she was very much a girl.

He moved to one side, pushing her down on the blankets as he took the gun away from her and kept one hand over her mouth.

"Will you be quiet if I take my hand off your mouth?" Jim asked her in a whisper.

She nodded. He relaxed his hand and as soon as it left her mouth she screamed. Jim went through the flap of the wagon and hit the ground running. He bolted away from the fire into the darkness. Martha's screams were mixed with crying now. He heard the boom of a shotgun but felt no pellets. A few pounding steps farther and he was in the darkness. He fell behind a sage bush and watched the camp. The fire grew brighter, then he heard the old woman calling into the darkness. She was on the other side of the wagon and he couldn't understand her. A few moments later she came to his side of the wagon and called into the night.

"Man? Deputy? If you can hear me, come on back. I got a good woman for you. She wants you, and she's got ten thousand dollars in gold coins in her trunk. Just waiting for you, man. Come on back, she's not so bad. Please come back, man!"

Jim began circling the wagon. Half way around he saw where Amy had tied his horse. He sat down and watched it. No one was near it. Not unless she were sleeping. He waited until the fire burned down and he saw two figures enter the wagon.

Jim looked at the stars and waited until it was almost midnight, then he moved cautiously toward his horse. He was sure no one was there. He moved as quietly as any Indian as he came up on the spot. Just as he reached for the reins which had been looped around a sage, he sensed someone behind him.

"Hello, Deputy, I've been waiting for you," Amy said.

She held out her hand and he grasped it.

"Thank you, Amy."

"Will you help me?"

"As long as they have the shotgun and rifle . . ."

"No, I meant help, *me.*"

"How?"

"Would you kiss me? I've never really been kissed before."

He held out his arms for her and she leaned against him. He bent down and touched her lips gently with his own, then pressed hard. She clung to him, holding him tightly, and when he released her she put her head on his chest and sighed.

"It really is fine, isn't it? Martha always tells me what wonderful feelings a kiss can begin. Then she goes on to tell me how she feels when she's making love. . . ."

She pushed away. "No, not again. That will last me for quite a while, I think."

Jim squeezed her hand. "When you get to Bisbee you'll find a young man who will make you very happy." He bent and kissed her cheek. "Now, I've got work to do. Tomorrow you find all of the shells for that rifle and shotgun and throw them out of the wagon. That Ma of yours could hurt somebody."

She still stood very close. "Amy, you sure you don't want me to kiss you again?"

"What? Oh, no. No thank you. I'm fine. And I heard about the ammunition. Good bye, Deputy. Maybe I'll see you again, when we get to Bisbee."

He checked the cinch strap, took the reins off the brush and mounted.

It took him half an hour to find the same spot he had used the previous night to watch the stage road. He dozed twice during the shank of the night, but no one moved down the trail.

He left his spot by the boulders just before the first false dawn and again was safely beneath the cedars before it was full light. He combed down the buckskin and rubbed him down before starting his smokeless cooking fire.

Jim was feeling groggy. He'd been up for almost forty-eight hours without any real sleep. Once he thought he saw a large blue-trimmed stagecoach rolling down the road. He blinked several times and the big coach evaporated.

Good strong coffee cleared his mind a little, and the breakfast helped even more. Two riders passed below him and one wagon, then the return trip of the stage and the road was clear again.

Just before noon he saw a tiny speck at

the far end of his view area. It seemed to be growing larger. He watched it as he ate again and drank all the water he could hold. An hour later the speck turned into a moving dot that billowed out a trail of smoke. It wasn't a stage; it was moving too slowly. He waited another hour and saw that the rig was still five miles down trail from him.

The next time he checked, the wagon was much closer and the volume of dust had increased, like the rig was speeding up. Now he could see that it was a covered wagon of some sort, but the top seemed overly high. It could be covering anything. When it came closer he saw one man riding on the front, high seat. Jim wished for a good pair of binoculars, the kind the officers had in the war. The only thing he could do without them was go down for a personal inspection. He saddled the buckskin and walked him down the hill, staying on the hard rock whenever possible, then taking a draw that would come out on the stage road behind the wagon.

When he jogged alongside the wagon a half hour later, he was dusty enough to satisfy anyone curious. The man on the wagon seat seemed old, in his sixties, Jim guessed. The wagon seemed normal enough as he came alongside it.

A big painted sign on the side read: *"Doc Methuselah and his magic-fountain-of-youth elixir."* There was a picture of a man on the wagon seat and printing under it that guaranteed he was a hundred and eighty years old.

Jim rode a little ahead of the wagon so he could turn and see the man clearly. Jim waved. As the old man on the seat saw Jim, he waved back, then slowly pulled the sturdy but unkempt looking team to a halt. When the dust settled from the big wagon wheels, Jim rode in.

"Howdy, you the Doc?"

"Why yes, yes, that I am, Doc Methuselah, now in my one hundred and eightieth year. What can I do for you, son?"

Jim had been watching the man. He certainly appeared younger than the sign said. But these medicine show guys were half actor half skinflint and half liar. His face was puffed yet windburned, an old straw hat pulled low over his eyes, and a kerchief half over his mouth. Pushing his kerchief down, he wrapped the reins around the end of the seat.

"Hanker for a snifter of something to settle the dust from your lungs, boy? I shore would." He reached through the opening behind him and came back with a bottle.

Instead of passing it to Jim the old man jumped agilely down from the high box and motioned Jim to the rear.

"Come on inside out of the damn hot sun." The man took the two steps built below the back of the wagon and jumped over the end gate, vanishing inside.

Jim followed him, tying his horse to the wagon. He went through the opening quickly, and let his eyes open up to give him the light they needed to see.

The inside of the wagon was fixed up more like a living room than a wagon. It had a drape on one wall, a sofa with cushions and blankets, even a small wash stand and a bucket of water. The old man was washing his hands and face.

"Got to stay clean, even in this bake-oven of a country. Where ye bound fer?"

Jim motioned on southeast. "Bisbee." He took the glass of whiskey the man poured him and sipped it. Straight. It was good whiskey.

"Suppose I could buy a bottle of that magic elixir from you, Doc?"

The old man chuckled and shook his head. "*Nosireeee*. Not a chance, boy. You come along just when I needed a body to jaw at. Fact is I might make camp right here and chew the rag with you all night. See,

I'm a talking man. Nothing I love more than to have about twenty galoots out front and put on my spiel about the good old elixir. But wouldn't sell it to a friend. It's good, been mighty good to me, kept me alive and out of jail for ten years now."

"Okay, Doc. This is good enough for me. Where you bound for?"

"Bisbee. Next stop. May put on a show there, depending how cooperative the sheriff is. Then might not. Might cut across above town and head on to Lordsburg. Now there's a town! I remember once I was there in sixty-one."

Jim tuned out the story and looked around the wagon, nodding, giving monosyllabic answers. The wagon was heavy, but looked about like the others he had seen doing this job. Most of them carried kegs of ingredients for the "magic" elixir that turned out to be mostly water, food coloring and a shot of whiskey. The better the talker the better the elixir.

The floor was covered with a carpet, a home woven model and made out of torn up strips of cloth providing a sturdy and practical rug. The floor had felt solid when he walked in.

After ten minutes of chattering with Doc Methuselah, Jim stood up.

"Thanks for the drink, but I better be moving on up the trail."

The old man's eyes narrowed for a moment. "What's the matter, you don't like the company?"

"No, no, nothing like that. I just got a little gal waiting for me up ahead, and I don't want her to worry I ain't coming."

They both laughed at that and Jim stepped outside and mounted. The old man's head came through the flap.

"Danged if I don't think I'll take a wee bit of a nap now that I'm stopped. No rush for me. Too blamed hot to travel anyway."

Jim waved and rode down the road toward Bisbee. Somehow he had the idea the man behind him was just what he seemed to be, but an irritating doubt nagged at him. He rode until a dip in the road put the wagon out of sight, then he turned and hurried up the draw toward Cedar Springs.

An hour later as he let the buckskin drink at the hole below the springs, the doubts came back with a rush.

He hadn't looked at the *bed* of that wagon. There could have been new planking under those rugs, with gold under them. The old man seemed remarkably spry for a person even sixty, and Jim remembered the way he had jumped down from the high wagon seat. Something was wrong with the setup, some final thing that could trigger his suspicions. He put his bedroll together, and stowed the rest of his food in the saddlebags. The old coot seemed anxious for Jim to hang around, stay all day. That wasn't unusual for these medicine men, they loved to talk and this one sure did. Wouldn't a man with a ton of gold be cold and suspicious of everyone? Jim cinched the saddle and wondered. What better camouflage, what better protection than a benevolent open-armness, a willingness to talk with everyone, to invite anyone into your "living room". Wouldn't it be a joke if the gold were right under his feet back there and he didn't know it?

Jim swung up on Hamlet and let him pick his way down the trail. The wagon had started moving again before Jim got to the wash. It was now well across his field of vision. Jim rode slowly, trying to think it through. Where had he missed? What one thing didn't he see?

He hit the main trail and still didn't know, but instinctively he knew something didn't ring true about old Doc Methuselah. The tracks were easy to find in the soft dust of the trail. He followed them at a walk for half a mile, then he stopped and stared at the ground in disbelief. Of course! It had been there all the time, and he hadn't seen it. In the road ahead was a low spot where the trail crossed a wash. The area harbored a small spring which kept the area continually moist. In the soft ground the wagon tracks had mired in deeply as they crossed the four foot span.

Jim got off his horse and looked at the tracks closer. The medicine show's wide wheels had sunk six inches into the mud and sand. Two feet farther over were the tracks of the stage coach from that morning. Its wheels had burrowed less than three inches deep.

A lot of weight on that wagon, Jim mused. Could it be a ton of gold under the false floor? He was sure that's what it had to be. The "old" man wasn't nearly as old as he seemed to be and the friendly open welcome he'd had was part of a carefully staged deception. One thing he knew for certain. There were no soldiers riding escort on this wagon, and none as out-riders. He had checked the surrounding territory carefully before he left the springs. There wasn't anothe ... e of a human being for twenty miles.

Jim swung back on the buckskin and jogged up the trail until he saw the plume of dust from the slow moving wagon, then he turned off the path and rode a mile across the desert toward the low ridge of hills. When he reached what he considered a safe distance, he paralleled the roadway again, keeping the heavily loaded wagon in sight. He felt better than he had in weeks. No big celebration was the right idea! Dan Barton had done everything but say the words for him. One man and one wagon. Who would think the army would get so tricky as to try anything like that? Send out a batch of decoy wagons, but push the real one through as a medicine man. Jim frowned as he remembered the "old" man in the wagon. He must be an expert, a real veteran and a master of all types of combat. The Doc would not be a man to take lightly when the showdown came.

For the rest of the day Jim trailed the wagon as it crawled across the barren land. Twice he caught himself veering too close to the trail and angled away. He had given up pacing the slower rig, instead rode ahead to high points and waited for the wagon to catch up. As he waited he ate, drank from his canteen and let Hamlet take a row. By nightfall they were still over ten miles from Bisbee.

Jim made a cold camp, tied Hamlet to a

193

scrub sage and hunkered down on a slight rise to watch the old man unhitch his team and let them rest. Jim wondered if the army man knew he was being followed. The odds were he did. Jim decided he should have stayed behind the wagon, letting the cloud of dust it kicked up serve as a smoke screen for him. But it was too late now. Tomorrow the rig would get to Bisbee. Would there be another change there? Would the medicine show wagon rumble into a barn somewhere, and when it came out look like a family covered wagon, or a minstrel show troupe, or maybe an empty freight wagon heading for the mines?

Jim left his horse and worked his way toward the wagon on foot, running down a draw, then crawling from bush to bush until he was two hundred yards from the wagon. No one was visible. Jim decided the old man was inside.

Suddenly a dozen shots rang out as six riders came in from behind the wagon and rode around it in a tight circle. Jim heard some words barked and the Doc came out the back of the wagon.

In the early dusk Jim couldn't be sure, but it looked like the fire-red beard of Red Paulson on the man who was directing the attack!

CHAPTER THIRTEEN

Jim tensed under the cover of the bush. How did Red Paulson tumble to the idea that this was the gold wagon? Or had he? As Jim watched Red got down from his horse and went inside with the Doc. A few minutes later they came out and Doc passed out a bottle to each of the men.

Red kept looking at the wagon. If he discovered the gold the old man wouldn't have a chance. Jim wanted to move closer, but there was no way. It wasn't dark enough to move without cover, and there was nothing to hide behind between where he was and the wagon.

Some of the men in front of him had dismounted and were pushing Doc Methuselah around. Nobody stopped them. Red kept looking at the wagon, at the huge kegs strapped underneath, at the fancy sign on the sides. The bottle he carried was larger than the others. He tilted it often in his inspection. At last he seemed satisfied.

It was getting darker. The men built a fire, and it soon became obvious Red and his crew would spend the night there. After the horses were picketed, the men unrolled blankets, threw more cactus wood on the fire and began cooking food.

Now Jim could work closer. When he found a slight dip in the ground he used it to worm his way within fifty feet of the fire. The men were eating. Red wasn't with them.

Jim heard only snatches of conversation and from it he gathered the men had not discovered the gold wagon yet.

Red came out of the wagon a few minutes later and bellowed.

"Pack up, you desert rats, we're moving out of here. Come on, let's go. Doc said he saw a wagon on the Lordsburg trail just before he turned off. We better check."

The men grumbled and cursed, but finished eating and packed their gear. Jim grinned into the blackness of the night. The pattern still fit. A friendly greeting, offer to stay the night by the gold wagon driver, then a clever way to get rid of them at the last moment. Jim was more sure than ever now that Doc was driving the gold wagon.

Red and his crew angled away from the

wagon northeast, cutting across the hills to meet the Lordsburg trail. When they were gone, Jim stood and dusted off his clothes, then walked back to the buckskin.

He slept cold that night, and dry, waking every two hours to be sure the gold wagon was still in front of him. He had been up two hours before the gold wagon began to move.

Jim knew he could take the wagon right there. Maybe that would be the smart thing, pick off the old man with his rifle, dispose of the body and drive the wagon into the hills where he could tear it apart, shoot the team and cover everything up but the gold. It could be his own private gold mine, coming back to get what he needed! But he didn't reach for the Sharps.

He'd never shot down a man except in a fair fight, and he decided he wouldn't start now. He'd killed a few men in his time, too many; there had to be a better way here. He wasn't sure if getting closer to Bisbee would be an advantage or a liability. It put the wagon closer to curious townspeople and travelers, but also closer to help if he needed any. His kind of help.

Before daylight Jim had saddled the buckskin and walked him toward the rim of hills to the north. The trail curved south ahead and skirted the hills. He wanted to be in them and well out of sight before Doc pulled by. He moved slowly in the darkness and when he came to the first rise four miles from the wagon, he let Hamlet take a breather as he rolled a smoke and watched the sun come up. The wagon was a black speck on the trail. He tied his mount behind a cluster of rocks and sat down beside another boulder. It would be two hours before the wagon got this far. The wagon still had almost five hundred miles to go before it hit a railroad spur. Almost anything could happen in five hundred miles by wagon.

Two hours later Jim woke with a start as a small lizard scurried over his hand. He let the creature dart behind the next rock, then raised up to look for the wagon. It was directly below him, and had been backed in off the trail in a U-shaped area of rocks. It looked almost like a fortified position.

Jim looked more closely. The team had been unhitched from the tongue and stood to one side. A pile of rocks showed under the near side of the wagon and as Jim watched, Doc came up with another boulder to add. A crude lever lay to one side.

"Dry wheel," Jim said out loud. Doc might be an expert on getting through hostile country, and know all about camouflage and deception, but he should have had that wheel checked at the last town. Greasing a wheel on a rig as heavy as that was not a one-man job. Jim picked up a stone and dropped it into the sand at his feet. Damn, why did he have to break down here? Doc went for another boulder.

Jim stood up. The wagon couldn't stay this close to the trail, so the wheel had to be fixed. He walked toward the rig, casually, and had slid the pry bar between the stack of rocks and the bed of the wagon when Doc came back.

"Well, now, where'd you come from?"

Jim leaned his weight on the heavy wooden timber and felt the wagon move upward a fraction of an inch.

"Going to need about a foot more of rocks," he said, sliding the timber to the ground. He adjusted the pile a little, putting up some rocks he had dislodged with the pole. "Greasing a wheel is not a one-man job, Doc. You should know that."

The old man's eyes softened and he nodded. "Much obliged," he said, looking closer at Jim. "Ain't you the gent I met on the trail yesterday?"

"Yep," Jim said and walked away to find another big rock. The old man came with him. He had his shirt off now and his bulging biceps looked more like those of a man of thirty.

"Wasn't you the one headed for Bisbee?"

"True." Jim said and turned. "But you'll never get there if you keep talking and not working. You remind me of the damned officers in the army, always talking and letting the men do the work." Jim looked up at the old man, watching him closely. He saw a sudden flare of anger in the man's eyes that was quickly controlled. So Doc was a soldier and an officer. That figured.

Five minutes later they had the rocks set and Jim eased the timber under the frame of the wagon, pushing down on the bar, then sitting on it to lift the wheel off the ground.

Next they let it settle back and found a rock to roll under the axle once they got it lifted.

It took a half hour of hard work to get the job done, but at last the offending axle and wheel had been separated. The axle was Arizona-dry.

"Where's your can of axle grease?"

Doc shook his head. "Don't have one."

"You'd make a hell of a teamster, Doc," Jim said. "How we gonna grease that axle without axle grease?"

The medicine man sat down and wiped his brow, scratching his scalp. "Truly I do not know, sir, truly."

"Got a slab of bacon in your supplies?"

"No."

"How about a cured ham?"

"No."

"Looks like you're stuck, friend. I'll stay with the wagon and you ride the eight miles into Bisbee for some grease."

"No ranches around here? How about the daily stage, maybe we could get some grease from them?"

Jim laughed. "Not a chance. They wouldn't even stop in here if a pair of naked women danced for them. Stage drivers call this bushwhack gulch. This is the favorite hold-up spot by outlaws."

"I can't leave my wagon, otherwise I'd accept your kind offer to stay while I ride to town. All of my elixirs and secret formulas, you understand?"

"I reckon."

"But say, why don't you ride to town for the grease? I'd be glad to pay you well."

"Pay? Hell, it'd take a half-million dollars to talk me into going to town."

Again Jim watched the Doc carefully. His eyes widened in surprise and this time he didn't recover so quickly.

"What do you mean by that?"

"You know what I mean, Doc, sir."

The other man stood and walked to the front wheel and back, turning and looking at Jim. "I don't have the faintest idea what you are speaking of, sir. As for payment, I could assure you twenty dollars for bringing back the grease. That's a month's wages in some parts!"

"You'd pay me in gold?"

There was a quick, involuntary jerking of Doc's head as he looked at Jim. His recovery was slower. "Why, yes, of course, a double eagle."

Jim pushed the medicine man down and dove behind a rock. He'd seen a flash of sun off metal in the rocks ahead of them, up the slope he had just left.

"Trouble," Jim said to the surprised Doc. "Somebody in the rocks back there. Get your rifle and pistol quick, and don't let them see you!"

Doc crawled past the wagon wheel like the soldier Jim knew he was, slit the canvas on the side away from the danger. A moment later he was back with two rifles and a six-gun. He had two boxes of army cartridges.

The first rifle shot slammed into a rock near them and whined away.

202

"Who are they?" Doc asked.

"I'd say Red Paulson and his gang, the ones you gave your magic elixir to last night just at dusk."

"You're the one who's been following me?"

"For a day or so, right after I saw those deep wheel tracks in the soft spot on the trail."

Four rifle shots slammed into the wagon then and both men lay close to the ground.

Doc took a quick look over the rock and snapped off a shot with the rifle, then dropped back.

"I don't know who you are, but I am authorized to pay a thousand dollars to anyone who helps me escape from a situation like this. Interested?"

"Authorized by the U.S. Army, correct?"

"Why, ah, yes."

"Okay, Captain, or Major, or whatever your rank is, that's enough of the pretending. I know you're army, I know this is an army wagon, and I know you've got a ton of gold hidden under that phony floor in there."

Jim drew his six gun fast and pointed it at the officer.

"You offer me a thousand to risk my life? Why? — when I can gun you down, call in

Red and split the gold fifty-fifty."

"Because you're no killer. You would have done that yesterday if you were going to. Oh, you'd like the gold, but you won't play it that way." Doc was checking the rocks, the wagon. "At least we've got a good defensive position here. It'll take a company to dig us out."

"Yes, and when they do we'll both be dead and they'll have the gold."

"They won't go far with it, it's in four-hundred pound bars," the officer said. He held out his hand. "Captain Frank Davis from Fort Brand."

"Jim Steel, from Bisbee and Kansas."

"You with me?"

"Four-hundred pound bars?

"Hell, I can't pack that in my saddle bags!" He took a shot at a movement above, then ducked down. "Lots rather see the army keep that gold than let Red Paulson get it."

He saw a man sprint down the slope toward a closer boulder. Jim lifted up and fired, the man tumbled into the dirt and lay still.

The attackers began to cover each other, some firing while others charged forward. Captain Davis picked off one more man but they had no idea how many they were facing.

Jim dug into the dust as a volley of shots came at them. He could almost taste the lead as it whined and bounced around them. Wiping the dirt off his lips, he moved to another rock and looked out. He jerked his head down quickly but there was no answering fire. This time he looked around the side of the rock and saw a pair of legs extending from the protection of a boulder fifty feet away. He sighted in and fired, watching the slug rip into the legs and bringing a howl of pain.

Jim saw a small smoke coming from behind a rock not thirty feet from where he lay. Smoke? He wondered about it. Then he noticed the dry grass around the rocks where they lay and around the wagon. The spring rains had brought up a fine crop, but now it was withered and dead — perfect fuel.

Jim brought up his six-gun, watching the rock. Whoever tried it would have to lift up to throw. There was no look, no warning, just a long, dry stub of a three-inch cactus stump burning fiercely, with an arm throwing it. Jim fired three times with the revolver at the arm but missed. He watched the burning brand as it hit the weeds and rolled. Immediately the grass and weeds caught fire, burning fiercely, eating toward them.

Captain Davis turned to Jim. "Fire, we've got to get out of here!"

"Where you planning to retreat to, Captain, everything's up or exposed to their rifles!"

"But that fire!"

Jim looked back at the flames, and for the first time he noticed the gentle breeze. It was blowing the flames and smoke away from them, back toward the attackers. Five minutes later the fire went out, having burned up the grass. Jim watched for another try, probably an attempt to circle or throw behind the wagon so the fire would burn toward it.

He saw a face sighting over the same rock as before and this time when the arm came up Jim was ready. He knew the man would have to throw farther, and come higher to get the distance. When the arm came up Jim sighted in where the man's shoulder should appear. His slug caught the man in the shoulder and slammed him down behind the rock before he could release the fire stick.

The attackers tried to burn them out twice more, but each time the throw fell short. Again a heavy concentration of fire came as they tried to get closer, but there was a broad open spot and none of the men tried to cross it.

Jim reloaded his six-gun during the lull and looked at the captain. He had his own revolver beside him and was checking his rifle.

"They waiting for darkness?"

"What would you do, Captain, if you were attacking us?"

"Get around behind us, crossfire."

As he spoke a man leaped from a rock, running quickly up the slope and slightly away from them. Jim laid out the territory.

"You take them going that way low, and I'll get the ones further back."

Captain Davis nodded and got his rifle into position.

In the next five minutes they wounded two of the five men who tried to circle behind them, and turned back the other two. The captain was an expert shot with his rifle.

Jim leaned toward the army man. "You want to get out of here alive?"

"I'm partial to staying alive — it helps your career," Davis said, grinning.

"If you don't mind taking orders from an ex-corporal, we can make it."

The captain laughed. "Right now, Jim, I'd take suggestions from the mess hall swamper."

Jim told him the plan, and the captain

nodded. They had been in front of the wagon during this time, with the attackers in front of them. They waited until they thought Red was ready to launch another attack and began pumping all the lead they could toward the other side. Soon a ripping answer came back with twenty shots. When it was quiet again Jim wormed his way between two rocks and under the wagon. As soon as he was there, Captain Davis came. Once on the other side of the wagon, they stood and ran for the rocks behind it. Using the wagon top to conceal their retreat, they worked halfway up the slope, before the next volley came from the other guns, but all the fire was aimed at the wagon.

They skirted a pair of huge boulders and were completely screened from the attackers. Jim brushed the sweat off his forehead and wished he had his canteen. It was on his horse, though, and that was on the other side of the hill.

Captain Davis loaded the empty chambers in his six gun, then looked up at Jim. "Now we get their horses, right?"

Jim gave his answer with a quick nod, turned and worked around the back of the hill at a slow trot. Halfway around Jim ran to the top of the slope and looked down the other side. None of the attackers had reached the wagon yet, but he saw one man scurry from one rock to a closer one. Jim spotted the horses, and ran back down the hill waving the captain to follow him. The eight horses had been tied well in back of the wagon, so the men had no trouble picking out a mount, then gathering up the reins of the other nags and leading them away. They hit the Bisbee trail at a gallop and soon were a mile from the sound of firing, heading for Bisbee and some help.

"You sure they won't have that gold out of the wagon and gone before we get back?" Jim asked.

Captain Frank Davis shook his head. "Not a chance. That false floor is bolted down every six inches around the sides. First they have to get through those bolts and two-inch oak planks, then they have to figure out some way to cut up those 400 pound gold bars."

"Okay, Captain, let's see if we can make these ponies break a sweat!"

He dug his spurs into the flank of the black he rode and galloped toward town.

CHAPTER FOURTEEN

"That's right, Mister. That's exactly what I said," Captain Davis said from his position standing on a chair in the Star and Garter. "I'll pay every man a hundred dollars for one day's work, fighting work. All you have to do is report in front of the sheriff's office in fifteen minutes with a rifle and thirty rounds of ammunition."

Ten men ran for the door.

A half hour later Jim and Captain Davis rode back toward the gold wagon with their rag-tag army. They had twenty eight men with good rifles, all eager for a short war, one that they knew they would win.

The rag-tags rode hard until they were a mile from the wagon, then the captain called a halt.

"Let's get this straight, men. You're in the army for today and you obey orders. If you don't, I have every right to shoot you dead. If I say advance, we do. When I say stop, everyone stops. When I say shoot, we shoot, and not until."

He looked around, noticing some surprised looks. "This isn't a hell-bent posse, we're an army doing army work. Now I want this gang and the wagon. We've got two objectives. Jim will take ten men and sweep around the far side to cut off the escape route. We'll move up as quietly as possible then ride in, shooting up everything we see."

He took off his hat and wiped his forehead. "You've heard about the massacre on the Broken Tree trail. This is probably the bunch that did it, so I'm not anxious to take any prisoners. Understood?"

He waved at Jim. "Take those ten men nearest you. We'll give you a fifteen minute start, then go in. Put your men in the rocks on the hill we went over."

Jim nodded and rode out. It took them a half hour to get where Jim wanted them, all hidden behind rocks but in sight of the wagon.

Jim watched below and now could see Red Paulson plainly, his bald dome shining in the sun. Men were whacking at the bed of the wagon with rocks. The rest of it lay scattered and torn apart. They had broken open every keg and carton looking for the gold.

Now they attacked the bed of the wagon with a lot of enthusiasm, but no tools. Jim saw five men working, two more lay in the shade of the rocks. At least two more must be dead in the rocks.

Suddenly from around the bend in the Bisbee trail less than a hundred yards from the wagon came Captain Frank Davis and his army. They rode in a long file, so each man could fire from his horse without hitting one of his own men.

The first sweep killed two of the wagon wreckers. Jim ordered his men to open fire. The second round of shots from the men on the hill cut down two more of the men below. Red Paulson jumped from behind the rock where he was hiding and began running toward the line of horses, both his six-guns spitting lead.

Jim raised his rifle at Red as a dozen other men did and the big red-beard jerked convulsively as bullet after bullet ripped into his body even as it was falling to the ground.

A minute later it was all over. Jim sent a man for their horses and walked down to the gold wagon.

None of the men had been told why the wagon was so valuable. They stared at the wagon, at the dead men. One of the Paulson gang was still alive. Captain Davis talked to him.

"What's your name?"

"Johnson, sir."

"Were you in the big war?"

"Yes, sir."

"Were you with Red Paulson when he ambushed that other wagon with twelve troopers on it?"

"Yes, sir."

Jim saw Captain Davis wince. The captain turned away, then looked down at the man. "My son was in that party, Johnson!"

The wounded man turned his head away. Jim started to jump for the captain but it was too late. He had pulled up his service revolver and pumped two bullets into the man's chest before anyone could move.

Jim turned away. He kept busy getting the wheel back on the wagon and the bodies loaded aboard. One of the wagon horses had been killed in the gunfire. It took ten men to get the harness off the dead horse. Then the single horse and an ex-plowhorse were teamed to drag the wagon into Bisbee.

Jim left the group, riding up the hill where he had left his buckskin. Hamlet stood at the same spot, pawing at the ground, switching his tail at the flies.

Jim scratched his neck and ears, then mounted and went back to the main party.

Something was bothering him, something about the gold wagon and its deep tracks, but he couldn't pin it down. He rode up to Captain Davis.

"Captain, if you need a witness about Johnson, I'll swear he was killed while trying to escape."

Captain Davis rode at the head of the column, his back stiff, one hand on the reins, the other on his leg, and he stared straight ahead. "That won't be necessary, Jim. The army takes care of its own."

For two miles, Jim tried to shake the idea that there was something he should have done that he hadn't. He thought back over the long chain of events that finally brought him to Bisbee to meet Aunt Abigail. The start of the end came on the Broken Tree trail a hundred years ago. . . .

As dusk began to settle over the trail Jim knew he had to go back to that first wagon. He wasn't sure why. He told the captain he was deserting the army, but maybe they would meet again before the wagon reached its final destination.

"I hope not, Jim. Because from here on we're going to have a hundred troopers around this hulk, and you couldn't get to it with half of Sherman's raiders."

"That would be interesting," Jim said,

saluted smartly and left the trail cutting cross country to the Broken Tree route. He rode slowly, trying to figure out why he had chosen to head for the site of the massacre at this time of day. He was half-way there when darkness closed in, but he kept moving. When he reached the site of the ambush, he found the wagon hulk but the moon had been covered up with clouds and he saw lightning. It wouldn't dare rain, not now. He studied the wagon in the darkness, then made a fire from the broken up boxes and looked at it again.

It hit him like the side of a sledgehammer. The floor, the bed of the wagon here was similar to that of the gold wagon! Both had what seemed to be a double floor that was bolted together!

Could there be *two* wagons, each with a ton of gold? No, that seemed impossible. The army wouldn't let this wagon sit here if there were anything valuable in it. Still, army messages, dispatch pouches, even messengers did get lost and misplaced.

He looked at the wagon bed in the glow of the fire. The top deck on the floor did look newer than the other. The bolts holding it on did seem to be brighter. What he needed was a good axe.

Instead Jim found a twenty pound rock

and began throwing it against the front edge of the wagon bed. It took a long time, and he was almost ready to wait until morning when the first floorboard behind the bolts broke, splintering downward. Down? It didn't punch through the bottom, so there had to be an opening, a hollow space!

He got on top of the wagon bed now, working at the point he had broken through and soon he had a space a foot wide smashed in. He pried the pieces out with a slat from one of the boxes.

The fire light wouldn't shine inside the opening, so Jim caught a burning board and held it low in the hole and looked inside. He sucked in his breath and looked again. There was no mistake, he saw the gleam of gold bars.

The first thrill of the find swept through him and then it was past and he settled down to work with the rock and pieces of the bed to pry with. An hour later he had half the box open.

So far he had discovered four bars of gold, each weighed around twenty pounds, he guessed. Around the sides of the gold bars were tough canvas bags. He opened one and found gold dust.

Jim wiped sweat from his face and looked at the dust. Money, more money than he had ever dreamed of owning. And he wasn't even stealing it! It was here for anyone who found it! Jim hefted the bag of gold dust. Ten pounds, maybe more. He counted ten of the bags, another hundred pounds of gold, and all his — all his and Dan Barton's, his army trooper spy.

He looked up for the stars to check the time, but the cloud cover was complete. He knew he couldn't leave the wagon like this. It had to be stripped clean by daylight. Jim kept working, building the fire higher with the wood from the wagon bed. After another two hours he had freed the last of the bags of gold and stacked them near the fire. What should he do with it all?

At the side of the gully he found where a large rock had been torn away, leaving a small cave-like area. It could work. Pile the gold dust in the depression, cover with big rocks and then pile high with dirt. Nobody would ever find it, except him when he was ready to use it.

Jim packed the gold dust away, mentally figuring what it was worth. At twenty dollars and sixty-seven cents an ounce, it would be worth more than three hundred dollars a pound! A hundred pounds would be more than thirty-thousand dollars. And he had almost two hundred pounds!

He took the four bars and put them in his saddle bags, throwing out most of the food to make room. He stood beside his buckskin looking at his work and smiling. Next, the wagon bed. He pushed the fire he had built under the near corner of it and knew that by morning most of it would have burned up, wiping out his mash job on it.

The soft night breeze had changed to a biting wind as he mounted up and rode back toward town. His mind was on the saddle bags. What did you do with a bundle of gold like that? Toss it to the hotel clerk and tell him to keep it? Or just toss it under your bunk and hope nobody looked inside? Jim rode from habit up to the sheriff's house. It had to be nearly morning. He wondered if Kathy would be awake. Jim knew which bedroom she had, since Luke used the front one. He went to the back window and tapped on it lightly, waited and tapped again. There was no response. He tried the back door and found it was open. Jim carried the saddle bags over his shoulder now and dropped them quietly inside the back porch on an old blanket. When he stepped into the kitchen he looked at the big wind-up alarm clock he had seen before. It was almost three a.m.

Jim looked at Luke's bedroom door a moment, then crossed and opened Kathy's. He stepped in quietly, closed the door and locked it before he went to the bed and knelt down in front of the soft quilts and the tousled head of Kathy. He kissed her cheek and she turned, making small sleep noises. Jim kissed her lips, tenderly, then, as she responded, more firmly, until her eyes came open slowly.

"Oh, darling, I didn't think you'd ever come," Kathy said. She reached around his head and pulled it back to her lips, kissing him hungrily. When her lips slid off his, at last, Jim took a deep breath.

"Kathy, are you awake?"

She smiled and sat up, letting the quilts and sheet fall away from her sleek, young body, and he smiled when he saw she wore nothing at all.

"Darling, I've been awake since your first tap on my bedroom window. Ever since you've been in town I've left that back door open, just hoping you'd come." She kissed him tenderly. "Now get out of those old clothes and come help me keep warm."

Much later when they woke up, she sat over him, twirling the black hairs on his chest.

"And so, darling, I decided that it was time I made up my mind about you. I had

219

to forget about you, or simply love you while you were here, before you rode away again, and left me with nothing but unfulfilled memories."

"We made no promises, no claims on each other, right?" Jim said.

"True. But I get a fair chance to prove to you that I can take care of you just as well as Adele or those other girls do." She smiled and lay down, pressing hard against him.

Jim frowned. Ever since he woke up he had been aware of some background noise, now it came louder.

"That noise, is that rain?"

"Yes, but it's outside, and we're in here, snug and warm. . . ."

Jim held up his hand for quiet. Now that he concentrated on it he knew it was rain, and not just rain but a real downpour.

Kathy sat up again, listening. "That's a real rain. It sounds like the way it did when we had that cloudburst."

Jim laughed, relieved to know what it was. He reached for the smooth fine body beside him. "I don't care if it's a regular old gully washer, if it washes out every stage coach trail this side of. . . ."

Jim stopped and sat up. His face a shocked mask of surprise and pain.

"Oh, no!" He stepped out of the bed and

grabbed at his clothes, pulling them on so fast he made mistakes.

Kathy frowned as she watched him.

"Whatever in the world . . . ?"

He seemed to notice her for the first time since he jumped up.

"It's raining. Every gully and ravine in the country will be hip deep full of water in an hour. So I've got a ride to make right now!"

Kathy looked at a locket type watch on her night stand.

"Jim it's five-thirty and it's pouring down rain. You're going to go riding now?"

"Yes, as soon as I get my boots on!"

"Then I'm going with you!" She jumped out of bed, pulled open drawers and began dressing. He started for the door, then stopped. It was always a treat for him to watch a woman dress, but right now he didn't have time.

"A horse?"

"I've got a bay in the shed out back. Saddle him up and I'll be ready by the time you are!"

Already she had on bloomers and was reaching for a wide, split skirt and a wrapper.

He went out the back door buttoning his coat, feeling the splash of the rain in his face. It felt as if someone had thrown a dozen buckets of water at him.

He saddled the small bay and was back at the door with the two horses quickly.

Kathy was waiting for him in the tiny porch, shivering. He hit his shoulder with his hand and watched the water splash.

"Come on out, the water's fine. You won't mind it a bit, once you're soaked to the skin."

"Where on earth are we going?"

"You'll see."

CHAPTER FIFTEEN

The rain came down by the gallon, it slammed into them in vertical walls, in sheets, it pounded in and around and through their jackets, sloshed inside their boots, puddled on their shoulders and dripped down their necks.

The rain was so hard they both were skin-wet in fifteen minutes. After that they almost forgot about being wet. But they couldn't talk. The howling wind continued to slant the giant drops at them, blinding them, slowing down the horses to a steady, sloppy walk.

Jim had headed out the Broken Tree trail, sticking to the middle of the track, but it soon turned into a river and he and Kathy cut to the side of the road following it through the rain in the early light of dawn.

For two miles they slogged through the mud, then returned to the road where it climbed the first grade. Here the water rushed past them down the incline.

Kathy shivered, she'd never been so cold, or wet or felt so bedraggled in her life. She had no idea what Jim was doing, but she'd made her decision about Jim Steel and from now on out she was going to spend every minute with him she could.

They kept moving up the trail, and when it narrowed the water came up to the bottom of their stirrups.

Jim kept them going, moving against the wind and rain, pressing forward as if his life depended on it. Every time the wind quieted so they could talk, Kathy asked him where they were going. He only shook his head at her and kept on moving.

When he came to a familiar looking hill he moved away from the trail and urged his mount up the side of the rocky, water-drenched slope. As they neared the top of the ridge, the rain slacked off, almost stopping.

Jim rode to the very top of the ridge and looked down.

"Down there, Kathy, is where the army men were bushwhacked. There used to be 12 graves down there, and part of an army wagon. But look at it now."

Kathy looked over the edge and saw only a boiling river, twenty feet wide that surged against the banks of the ravine, sweeping everything in front of the angry water. The water was dirt brown tearing at the banks as it roared downstream.

"Must be five, six feet deep out there," Jim said. He swung down from the horse and sat down on the wet ground, staring at the water. "You asked me why I came out here, still want to know?"

She dismounted and sat beside him. "Yes, Jim. I want to know."

So he told her all about it. About Dan Barton and how he found out about the army gold going through, how they narrowed down the trails and at last pinpointed it through Bisbee. He put it all out for her to see. After he told her about the gold in the first army wagon he pointed to a sage bush.

"See that sage right there, the one with the twisted top? Well right below that I planted over thirty-three thousand dollars in gold, gold dust!"

"Dust! But the water . . ."

"Right. That's the richest blasted flood water you'll ever see."

"But some of it might be there. Couldn't we look?"

He nodded. "We can look, but that's all the good it's going to do us. The water

225

blasted everything away in front of it. There must be gold dust all the way to Mexico City by now."

They jogged down the hill the way they had come up and a quarter of a mile on the flat found a place they could cross the wash with only their boots dragging in the water. On the other side they spurred back to the ambush site.

The rain had stopped now, but the water rumbled and roared as it surged past the spot. Jim walked down to the edge of the water and put his hand in the water and brought it up. There were flecks of gold still in the water. He found the exact spot easily and waded into the side of the brown flood. It dropped sharply. Jim felt his feet hit a rock. That surprised him, he thought they all would be washed downstream.

Quickly he took off his hat, his wet coat and wet shirt and dropped into the water where he had stood. He felt the muddy water pulling at him, but his hands investigated around the base of the rock. For just a moment he thought he touched the softness of canvas. He had to come up gasping for breath.

Kathy was beside him wiping the mud from his eyes, then her eyes went wide. His whole torso was covered with thin flakes of pure gold. He took three huge lungs full of air, then splashed back into the water. His hands closed tightly around the canvas sack top and pulled, but nothing budged. He tried to push the rock but it was stuck tightly, then he had to get up for air.

He sat on the bank this time, resting, getting his body filled with new oxygen.

"Think I've found something, maybe one left," he said in a quick burst of words. He looked at the problem again, and this time he went upstream a yard before he sunk below the muddy tide. He would push with the current, let it help him move the rock. Once more he caught the top of the canvas bag and, now pushing with the current, felt the rock move. Twice more he lunged against the rock and the last time it rolled, tilted and was swept away. The canvas bag came free and he felt the weight of it plainly. He made sure the top was tightly closed then came to the surface before his lungs burst.

He crawled out of the water lying on top of the gold dust and panting to catch his breath. When he rolled over and sat up Kathy sat beside him. He picked up the sack of gold and put it on her lap. She didn't notice the mud, only looked inside at the muddy, soaked gold dust.

"Is it real?"

"Good as gold," he said. "Wait until it's dried out a little. Then you'll never see anything prettier."

He looked at the water, and saw that his feet were still in the muddy flow.

"I better look again, there might be one more," he said touching her shoulder. He dropped into the water and felt all around where the gold had been, but there were no more big stones, and no more gold bags.

He lay on the bank for fifteen minutes, then put on his shirt and coat. Kathy was still looking at the gold.

"It's hard to believe this is worth so much. Over twenty dollars for an ounce?"

"Yes. If there's ten pounds there that sack is worth over three thousand dollars."

She gasped. "That much?"

"Maybe a little more."

They rode slowly back toward town, watching the muddy flow. Nearly a mile down the wash they found one of the gold sacks. It was nearly empty, but Kathy insisted they take it with them. She put her hand in the water and brought it up, admiring the flecks of gold.

She watched Jim. "You in a hurry to go somewhere?"

"First to your place for a bath and some

dry clothes, and about a mile-high stack of hot cakes."

"But tomorrow? Will you be here tomorrow?"

"Remember last night? We said no strings, no promises?"

"I remember."

"Tomorrow I'll be riding west."

"Phoenix?"

"I have to find Dan Barton. He's due his half."

"Jim, I'll ride wherever you ride. I'll go with you!"

He shook his head. "No life for a woman. Wait me out. I'll come back and settle down, maybe even run for sheriff, but not now."

"So you'll ride off from me again?"

"You knew it all the time. You set your hat for the richest single man in Bisbee and I guarantee you'll land him. You can do almost anything you set your mind to."

He motioned to the sack of gold dust he carried. "This is my wedding present to you. Your dad will know what to do with it. We'll have the army canvas sacks burned long before Luke sees them. Put the dust in a good tin can and keep it till you need it."

Jim began to whistle in the early morning sunshine. He'd be gone before the day was dried out, with clean clothes and a loaded warbag and those saddle bags with their eighty pounds of yellow. It made him feel good that he was moving on, out into the country where no one knew him and he knew no one, where he could live life on its own terms and let the best man win. The gold? It would come in handy. He'd put it in a bank in Phoenix or Denver, maybe even San Francisco. It would be waiting there when he needed it.

They reined up at the back door of Luke's house and both got down stiffly. He'd talk Luke into staying on as sheriff. No reason not to now that Red Paulson was dead and Duke Jannis was around to help him with the rough types. Ed Percival wouldn't cause any trouble for a while. He'd see how the wind was blowing and stay out of trouble.

As soon as Jim opened the rear door they heard Luke yelling.

"Kathy? That you? Where the hell have you been? You missed the excitement. The gold wagon got here and the posse killed Red Paulson. Kathy! That you? Get in here and make me some breakfast. Damn, I think I'll go down to the office today."

Kathy looked sadly at Jim, shrugged, and without bothering to take off her muddy clothes, went into her father's bedroom.

Jim peeled off his jacket and shirt and put water on the stove to heat. He was anxious to get cleaned up, and back on the trail to find Trooper Dan Barton.

The employees of Thorndike Press hope you have enjoyed this Large Print book. All our Thorndike and Wheeler Large Print titles are designed for easy reading, and all our books are made to last. Other Thorndike Press Large Print books are available at your library, through selected bookstores, or directly from us.

For information about titles, please call:
   (800) 223-1244

or visit our Web site at:
   http://gale.cengage.com/thorndike

To share your comments, please write:
Publisher
Thorndike Press
295 Kennedy Memorial Drive
Waterville, ME 04901